Chestnut Hill
A Time to Remember

Lauren Brooke

■SCHOLASTIC

*With special thanks to
Catherine Hapka*

Scholastic Children's Books
An imprint of Scholastic Ltd
Euston House, 24 Eversholt Street
London, NW1 1DB, UK
Registered office: Westfield Road, Southam, Warwickshire, CV47 0RA
SCHOLASTIC and associated logos are trademarks and or
registered trademarks of Scholastic Inc.

First published in the UK by Scholastic Ltd, 2008

Copyright © Working Partners, 2008

ISBN 978 1407 10485 0

British Library Cataloguing-in-Publication Data
A CIP catalogue record for this book is available from
the British Library

The right of Lauren Brooke to be identified as the author
of this work has been asserted by her.

Printed by CPI Bookmarque Ltd, Croydon, CR0 4TD
Papers used by Scholastic Children's Books are made from
wood grown in sustainable forests.

5 7 9 10 8 6 4

www.scholastic.co.uk/zone

Chapter One

"Enter at A, halt and salute at X, then track right at C," Lani Hernandez muttered. "Or wait … was it *left* at C? Aargh! Why can't I remember the stupid test?"

Lani was leaning on the fence of one of Chestnut Hill Academy's outdoor riding rings, staring at the rectangular dressage arena that had been laid out inside. The dressage test was the opening phase in the first-ever Combined Event to be held at Chestnut Hill; the new cross-country course would have to be completed next, and finally a round of show jumps at the end of the day. Crisp black letters on white boards marked eight points around the arena – three on the long sides and one each on the shorter sides – where transitions and movements had to take place.

Everyone around Lani was getting ready for their turn in the ring, but she wasn't moving until she had cracked this test. She narrowed her eyes to look at the judge's table at the far end, where a rather stern-looking woman was drinking coffee. A Chestnut Hill senior sat beside her, acting as a scribe and scribbling notes about the seventh-grader from one of the visiting schools who was just leaving the ring.

Lani's friend Malory O'Neil looked up from adjusting her riding boots and blew a strand of curly dark hair out of her face. "You start off tracking *right*," she told Lani. "The walk-trot test for the Starter class goes to the left. You should stop watching them ride – you'll only get confused."

"She's right." Lani's best friend and roommate Honey Harper was standing nearby watching a couple of riders warming up in the next ring. She bit her lip, an anxious expression flitting across her heart-shaped face.

"What's up?" Lani asked.

"I'm just wondering whether I should have tried entering the Starter class rather than attempting Open on my first time out."

"Don't sell yourself short, Honey," Lani told her firmly. "You used to do one-day eventing back in England, right? I'm sure you and Minnie will do great."

"Oh, it's only me I'm worried about." Honey smiled, brushing back her blonde hair. "I know Minnie will be wonderful."

Her expression softened, as it always did when she mentioned Moonlight Minuet, better known as Minnie. Honey loved the pretty, affectionate grey mare just as much as Lani adored Colorado, the dun gelding that she rode whenever she could.

For a while, it had looked like Honey would lose Minnie for ever, as one of their classmates Patience Duvall, the grey mare's owner, was determined to sell her.

2

Lani knew that the idea of losing Minnie had been close to unbearable for Honey, as she had already said goodbye to her first pony, Rocky, when her family had moved from England to the United States a year before.

Then their friend Dylan Walsh had stepped in. Lani still grinned whenever she thought about it. Dylan was known for being impulsive and generous – but she was also known for being a first-class schemer! All those qualities had come together in the plan she'd concocted to keep Honey and Minnie from being separated. Dylan's parents had offered to buy her a show horse, but Dylan had decided she wanted to keep working with Morello, the lively skewbald gelding she normally rode at Chestnut Hill. So instead, she had convinced her parents to invest their money in Minnie and offer her to Honey on a long-term lease.

"Did I miss my turn?" someone called breathlessly.

Lani looked over to see her classmate Tessa Harding racing past, her competitor's number trailing from the pocket of her jacket and her curly brown hair escaping from beneath her helmet. She had a slightly panicky look on her face.

"Don't worry, you've got one more to go before you. Good luck, Tessa!" Lani called, though she wasn't sure the other girl even heard her. Tessa was riding in the first Open group, which meant Lani's ride time was coming up as well. That reminded her – what the heck was she supposed to do after that first twenty-metre circle?

A seventh-grader named Joanna Boardman rode

past on her own pony, a cute bay Welsh cross named Calvin. Both pony and rider looked tense, and Calvin even let out a whinny to a horse on the far side of the arena, though he settled into a steady trot as soon as he entered the warm-up ring. Meanwhile, a group of three girls dressed in the hunter-green jackets of Two Towers Academy hurried past, leading their horses behind them.

Malory came and stood beside her, staring around the yard. "I still can't believe that this event came together so fast."

"I know what you mean," Lani said. "For a while it seemed like we'd *never* get to try out the cross-country course!"

At the start of term she had been eager to sample the new permanent fences that had been built on the school grounds the previous spring. However, a bout of heavy rain – the remnants of a hurricane passing up the coast – had left the ground too soft. With the excitement of adjusting to being eighth-graders and everything else that went along with the new school year, Lani and her friends had almost forgotten about the as-yet-unused cross-country course.

But finally things had dried out enough. Lani remembered how amazing it had been the day she and her friends had arrived for their riding lesson and the Director of Riding, Ali Carmichael, had announced that they'd be trying out a few cross-country jumps that day. As Lani had expected, she and Colorado had taken to cross-country like ducks to water. The sturdy dun pony had pricked his ears as they'd approached the first obstacle, an inviting elementary-height log, at a brisk trot. He'd sprung over the small log with at least a foot to spare! He'd attacked the next obstacle, a stone wall, with equal enthusiasm. A few times Ms Carmichael had even asked Lani to lead a couple of the less-confident ponies over a jump.

That lesson had been just over a week ago, and was swiftly followed by the announcement of the mini-event, with several local schools invited to make the competition even tougher.

"It's no wonder I can't remember my dressage test," Lani said. "We've only been practising it for a week and a half!"

"You know what Mr Musgrave says," Malory reminded her, referring to their strict but knowledgeable dressage instructor. "We're not supposed to practise the test itself. Otherwise the ponies learn the sequence of movements and start to anticipate."

"Fair enough," Lani countered. "But I'm pretty sure even Mr Musgrave would agree we are supposed to learn the test ourselves!" She glanced at the dressage arena again and frowned. "How do you guys remember it, anyway? Did you have the test tattooed on your horses' necks or something?" She brightened. "Hey, that's not a bad idea – anyone have a marker pen?"

Honey laughed. "Actually, I use a tip from my instructor back in England."

Before she could reveal the secret, Dylan came

rushing up, her red hair flying and her green eyes wide and panicky. A bridle was dangling over her shoulder, the reins dragging behind her and threatening to get tangled up with her spurs.

"Have you seen Morello?" she panted.

Malory stared at her in surprise. "What do you mean? Haven't *you* seen him?"

"Don't tell me you managed to lose your pony!" Lani exclaimed, reaching down to grab Dylan's reins and loop them back over her shoulder. "That's pretty bad even for you, Walsh!"

"I know!" Dylan moaned. "I'm absolutely positive I left him tied up outside the barn while I went to clean off his bit, but he seems to have turned into Soda!" She grabbed the bridle off her shoulder and shook it at her friends, as if to ward off any further argument. "Now, call me crazy, but I think I can tell the difference between a 14.1-hand piebald and a 15.3-hand palomino…"

Kelly Goodwin, one of Chestnut Hill's stable hands, hurried past in time to hear her. "Don't panic, Dylan," she said calmly. "I took Morello back to his stall to keep him out of the way. He was trying to untie his lead rope, and I didn't want him wandering around getting into trouble."

"Oh, thank goodness!" Dylan cried. "See? I knew I wasn't going crazy!"

"That's debatable." Lani grinned. "Only a crazy person would leave Morello tied up on his own like that. Everyone knows he's an escape artist."

"OK, so you've located your pony," Honey said as

Dylan stuck out her tongue at Lani. "But I think you may have lost something else." She shot a meaningful look at Dylan's arm. "Where's your medical card?"

Lani glanced at the armband on Dylan's arm, which was empty. She patted her jacket pocket to make sure her own armband and medical card were still there. Over the past week or so, they had learned a whole new set of rules and regulations related to eventing. For instance, they all had to wear hard protective vests during their cross-country rounds, and an armband containing their medical information during both jumping phases.

Dylan glanced down and groaned. "The stupid thing keeps slipping out!" she said. "It probably fell off in the wash stall again. I just hope it didn't get soaked this time – it's already kind of smudged..."

"Relax. I'll help you find it." Malory checked her watch. "You're not riding until group three anyway, right? Me too. That gives us plenty of time to track down your card."

Dylan didn't answer. Her eyes had narrowed and she was staring at something over Lani's left shoulder. Lani turned and followed her gaze towards the bleachers outside the far end of the ring. There were several dozen people gathered there waiting to cheer on the riders, but Lani guessed right away which ones in particular had caught Dylan's attention.

Malory glanced over too. "Check it out," she said. "Looks like Lynsey and Patience are making some new friends."

Lynsey Harrison and Dylan were roommates that year, to their mutual dismay. The only thing the two of them had in common other than their room number was an interest in fashion.

And they can't even agree about that, Lani thought as she watched the tall, slender blonde girl throw back her head and laugh at something the guy next to her had just said. Nearby, Patience was chatting with another guy. Both girls were wearing Seven jeans and Prada boots, which stood out among the sea of riding clothes and school colours all around them.

"Who are those boys Lynsey and Patience are talking to?" Honey wondered aloud.

"I don't know," Dylan replied, slapping the bridle she was holding against her boot. "But I know one thing. Neither of them looks like Lynsey's alleged boyfriend, Jason!"

"Duh," Lani joked. "Jason has no interest in horses. How can you expect Lynsey to go without male attention for an entire day?"

Dylan rolled her eyes. "Well, she could have distracted herself by entering the event instead of being so snobby about it, for starters."

Lani grinned. "But you heard what she said. Poor, precious Blue might chip a nail ... er, hoof!"

Lynsey had brought her own pony to Chestnut Hill ever since the start of seventh grade. Bluegrass was an impeccably bred and well-trained blue roan gelding with a list of A-circuit championships a mile long. Personally, Lani thought Blue would probably have a blast galloping around the cross-country course instead of being stuck in the ring all the time. But Lynsey clearly considered eventing a second-class sport and wanted to make sure everyone knew it. Then again, Lani was used to that sort of thing from Lynsey. From the moment the snooty girl had discovered that Lani had done almost as much Western riding as English, she'd taken every possible opportunity to pour scorn on that, too.

"At least Lynsey came to cheer us on," Honey said.

Lani smiled at her. That was typical Honey – she always tried to see the best in everyone.

"To cheer us on?" Dylan said. "Or to flirt with cute boys from Saint Kit's?" She let out a snort. "I mean, come on – those guys have to be tenth-graders at least! In fact…" Her voice trailed off and she marched off toward Lynsey and Patience.

"What's she doing?" Malory sounded worried. "She doesn't have time to get in a fight with those two right now – not if she wants to find her medical card, watch you two ride and still get Morello warmed up in time."

Even from across the ring, Lani had no trouble hearing Dylan as she loudly greeted Lynsey and Patience as if they were her best friends. Both girls shot her annoyed looks, but that didn't stop her.

"So what did you guys think of that history test we had yesterday?" Dylan practically shouted, attracting the attention not only of Lynsey and Patience and their cute neighbours but most of the other spectators as well.

"Looks like we're going to have to work a lot harder now that we're all in *eighth grade*, huh?"

Lani grinned, suddenly realizing what Dylan was up to. The two Saint Kit's boys looked rather alarmed; it was obvious Lynsey and Patience had let the boys think they were older than they really were, with their high-end clothes and confident manner. Within seconds, both of them were pushing away through the crowd, leaving a pair of very disgruntled-looking Seven-wearing eighth-graders behind.

Before Lynsey and Patience could react, Dylan scooted off in the direction of the barn.

"I'd better go help her find that card," Malory said. "But don't worry, we'll be back to see you guys ride."

As she hurried away, the PA system crackled to life. Ms Carmichael's voice floated out over the grounds. "The last of the dressage tests for the Starter group has taken place. Riders in this group can now proceed to the cross-country course according to your times. Meanwhile, we'll shortly be getting started with the first Open group's dressage. Please take note of your ride times and be ready to go when your name is called."

Lani felt a flutter of panic. The countdown had begun and she still wasn't ready! "So, Honey, about that memory tip you were talking about..." she prompted.

"Oh, right!" Honey picked up her riding crop, which had been leaning against a fence post. "You just draw the test like this..." She sketched a rectangle in the dusty ground. "Pretend the end of this crop is your horse, so enter at A…" She drew a line straight up the centre, and then traced a circle around to the right to indicate the pattern for the test. "See? That way you don't have to worry so much about remembering the letters. You just learn the pattern and changes of pace from a bird's-eye view."

"That's a great idea!" Lani exclaimed, borrowing Honey's stick and having a go. "It makes the whole thing sort of like geometry. I should be better at this than I am at memorizing a random bunch of letters." She glanced up at the dressage ring and wrinkled her nose. "If they had to use letters, why couldn't they at least pick ones that made sense? I mean, I don't care how many little rhymes Ms Carmichael tries to teach us – I'll never be able to remember A-K-G-H!"

"It's A-K-E-H, actually," Honey corrected her. "But I know what you mean." Suddenly her face lit up with a smile. "Oh, look, my family made it! Over here!" She waved.

Crop still in hand, Lani turned to see Honey's twin brother, Sam, and their parents approaching. Sam reached them first. Lani stared at him, surprised by how well he looked. He'd spent the past year fighting off leukaemia, and only within the past month had he been officially declared in remission. He was still too thin, but his blond hair was growing back and his skin had lost the sickly pallor caused by too much time spent indoors. It now had the same healthy glow as Honey's.

He looks amazing! Lani thought. *The way Honey talks,*

I was expecting him to look really ill. She's always saying how he's still weak and that it will take a lot longer for him to recover.

"Taking up a new art form, are you, Lani?" Sam enquired, peering down at her scratchings on the ground. "Hmm. I wouldn't say that it reminds me of da Vinci. Picasso, maybe..."

Lani grinned at him. Her sense of humour had clicked with Sam's from the first time they'd met. Even though they didn't see each other very often, they always seemed to pick up right where they'd left off.

"Hey, what can I say?" she retorted. "Some of us have hidden talents."

"Yes. And some of us have talents that ought to *stay* hidden," he joked, returning her grin.

Honey rolled her eyes and poked her brother on the arm. "Be nice," she chided. "Lani's in a panic about her dressage test. She's due to ride in a few minutes."

Lani checked her watch and gulped, realizing Honey was right. "Yikes," she said. She shot an apologetic smile at Honey's parents, who had just caught up. "Hi, Mr and Mrs Harper. It's good to see you but I have to run!"

"Yes, we'd better go get the ponies." Honey smiled at her family and gestured towards the stand at the side of the arena. "You guys can sit over there to watch."

"The best seats in the house," Mr Harper joked.

Sam nodded. "Good luck, sis," he said. "You too, Lani. Not that you'll need it – Honey's always saying what a brilliant rider you are."

"Um, thanks." Lani was surprised to find herself

blushing. Turning away to hide her confusion, she grabbed Honey by the hand. "Come on," she said. "If Chestnut Hill is hosting this event, we'd better make sure we show up on time!"

Chapter Two

Easy, easy, Lani thought, half-halting as she rode Colorado into the corner. *Not too fast, now…*

It was tempting to say it out loud – Colorado responded well to voice aids. But Mr Musgrave had told them that using the voice was forbidden in a dressage test and would get them marked down.

Instead she half-halted again, supporting the pony's inside shoulder and keeping her leg on to prevent him from leaning in too much on the turn. They rounded the corner nicely and headed up the centre line for the last time. Taking in a breath, Lani tried to gauge exactly where to signal for the halt. The letter X was located in the exact centre of the ring, although unlike the others it wasn't marked; Dylan liked to call it the "invisible letter", and pretended that it had slipped out for a soda while they weren't paying attention and that was why she hadn't halted Morello in quite the right spot…

Lani realized she was smiling as she thought about Dyl goofing around. Snapping back to the here and now, she gave a light half-halt to prepare Colorado for the transition; then, when she was pretty sure they were in the right spot, she sat deeper and asked for the halt. The gelding came to a square stop immediately.

Lani grinned, so pleased with the prompt transition that it took her a second to remember that she was supposed to salute the judge. Grabbing both reins in her left hand, she swept her right arm down to her side and nodded. The judge nodded back and smiled, then turned to say something to her scribe for the current division, Chestnut Hill ninth-grader Tanisha Appleton.

Taking a deep breath, Lani let the reins go slack and leaned forward to give Colorado a big pat with both hands. "Good boy," she whispered. "And thank goodness for Honey's stick-in-the-sand trick. Otherwise I never would have remembered all that!"

Lani realized that the judge was smiling at her. Ms Carmichael had explained that since this was an informal event, the judges might be willing to give them some tips after their performances. Lani nudged Colorado forward. Tanisha glanced up long enough to give her a smile and a thumbs up, then returned to scribbling notes on Lani's test sheet.

"Nicely ridden," the judge said when Lani was close enough. "Your pony has lovely gaits, and your test was quite accurate. Next time, think about keeping him straighter on your diagonals, and try to make your transitions from canter to trot smoother."

"I will," Lani promised. "Thanks!"

She turned to ride out of the ring, wondering what the judge would say if she knew that Lani had only

15

learned the test about twenty minutes earlier. Leaning forward, she patted Colorado again.

"My secret is safe with you, right, buddy?" she whispered.

Soon Colorado was tucked in his stall to rest up for the cross-country phase. Lani hurried out of the barn, hoping she hadn't missed Honey's ride. She found her friend just finishing her warm-up with Dylan and Malory watching from the rail. Glancing over towards the main ring, Lani saw that a girl from one of the other schools had just started her test on a tall chestnut gelding.

"Good job out there, Lani," Malory said when Lani joined them. "Colorado looked great!"

"He *was* great, wasn't he?" Lani felt herself swell with pride. "I mean, he's never going to be as smooth as silk like Minnie or as crisp in his transitions as Tybalt. But I don't think we disgraced ourselves."

Just then Honey spotted her and rode over to the rail. "You looked fantastic out there, Lani," she said.

"Thanks." Lani could tell that her friend was nervous. "Now it's your turn. Go out there and put me to shame!"

Honey gulped. "I don't know about that," she said. "I'm just hoping I don't faint and slide off halfway through!"

After giving her a few more assurances, Lani and the others hurried over to the viewing area. Honey's parents were sitting in the stand chatting with some other adults, but Sam was standing at the rail.

"Honey's up next," Lani told him, pushing in beside him. "Get ready to cheer."

"I'm ready." Sam's fingernails dug into the wooden fence board. "I just hope Honey's OK. She gets so worried sometimes about messing up that she psychs herself out."

"Don't worry," Dylan assured him. "Minnie's a pro. She'll take care of her."

"That's right," Lani said. "Honey is the star of Mr Musgrave's class, and Minnie dances like a dream."

"She's not supposed to be dancing," Sam quipped, though he still looked anxious.

Honey's face was white and pinched and her shoulders looked rather stiff when the bell rang for her to begin her test. But as soon as she and Minnie trotted up the centre line, she seemed to relax. The two of them went on to turn in a lovely, smooth test. Every transition was right on target, and Minnie's paces had never looked better. By the time Honey gave her final salute, she was beaming.

"Whoo-hoo!" Dylan hooted as soon as the judge returned the salute. "Way to go, Hon-*neeeeee*!"

"Yee-haw!" Lani whooped.

A handful of seniors from their dorm were standing a little further down the rail. They looked over and grinned. Helen Savage let out a loud wolf whistle. "Adams dorm rules!" she shouted.

Rachel Goodhart and Rosie Williams pumped their fists in the air. "Yeah, Honey!"

Honey shot her cheering section a glance, her cheeks

going red as Sam and Malory added their shouts as well. She gave them all a little wave, then rode forward to get her comments from the judge.

"Wow, she made that look easy," Malory said admiringly.

Lani nodded. "So much for the rest of us," she joked. "Honey has this one in the bag."

"Not so fast," Dylan protested. "Mal and I haven't even ridden yet! Besides, we've still got the two jumping phases to go."

"Why did you have to remind me?" Lani groaned. "I'd just forgotten to be nervous!"

"I don't know what you have to be nervous about," Dylan retorted. "Colorado could probably jump that whole cross-country course backwards!"

Sam raised one eyebrow. "That doesn't sound too safe." He shrugged. "Then again, I suppose it would be less scary if you couldn't see the jumps coming."

Malory laughed. "Come on, Dyl," she said. "We'd better go start warming up."

The two of them said goodbye and headed for the barn. Lani glanced toward the ring, where a boy from Saint Christopher's Academy, better known as Saint Kit's, had just entered on a striking leopard Appaloosa.

"OK, I don't have to start warming up for cross-country for half an hour," Lani told Sam. "How are you going to distract me from getting nervous until then?"

"Well, let's see." Sam pretended to think hard. "I know! How about some lunch? Mum packed a huge picnic basket."

Lani made a face. "Hmm, that might not be such a good idea," she said, patting her stomach. "Nerves plus food in stomach could equal bad news."

"No, really. Wait here a sec." Sam turned and sprang up the bleachers towards where his parents were sitting.

Lani watched him, impressed again by how much better he seemed. Anyone who didn't know he'd just battled cancer would never guess it seeing him now. She liked to consider herself a pretty brave person, but she wasn't sure she could have bounced back as quickly as he had, sense of humour intact.

Soon Sam returned dragging a wheeled cooler. "*Voilà!*" he said, opening the lid. "We have chicken salad, rolls, coleslaw, home-made chocolate cake..."

Lani had been shaking her head until he got to the last item. "Wait, did you say chocolate cake?" she said. "Hmm, actually, that might just help settle my stomach – and are those muffins?"

"Apple muffins," Sam replied. "Mum's speciality."

"Well, I really wouldn't want to be rude..." Lani grabbed one of the muffins while Sam cut them each a generous slice of the cake.

"Don't look up at Mum and Dad," he warned as he handed it over. "They're the old-fashioned sorts who disapprove of eating dessert before lunch."

Lani laughed. "Get real," she said. "I mean, maybe they'd disapprove for *me*. But they're probably so thrilled that you have your appetite back that they'd let you eat cake and ice cream for every meal!"

"Good point." Sam grinned. "Come to think of it, it *was* my idea to include both the cake and the muffins today."

For the next few minutes, Lani and Sam ate and chatted and watched the riders in the ring. Lani had always gotten along with boys just as well as she did with girls. Still, it was a little amazing to her just how easy it felt to hang out with Sam.

Then again, why should I be surprised? she thought, licking chocolate icing off her fingers. *Sam is Honey's twin, and Honey is one of the coolest and most fun people I know. It makes sense that Sam should be equally awesome!*

Finally she spotted Dylan riding into the arena on Morello. "Oops," Lani said with a twinge of guilt. "I meant to go over and help Dyl and Mal warm up."

"Never mind." Sam closed the cooler lid and stood up, brushing the crumbs off his hands on his jeans. "Dylan looks ready to go regardless."

That much was true. Dylan could be a bit scatty, and it sometimes showed in her personal appearance – like the time she'd showed up for a riding class wearing one paddock boot and one designer loafer, insisting that she must have left her paddock boot in the arena the day before, or the numerous times she'd almost left for breakfast still wearing her bedroom slippers. Morello was her kindred spirit in this, as he was in most other things. He was famous for finding just the right puddle or pile of manure to roll in to dirty the white sections of his skewbald coat. But at the moment, they both looked like a million dollars. Dylan's boots shone, her jacket and breeches were spotless, and her red hair was fully contained inside her helmet. Morello was equally immaculate, his white parts gleaming and his brown-and-white mane neatly plaited.

Lani crossed her fingers as the bell rang and Dylan began her test. But she needn't have worried. The pair laid down a performance almost as smooth and professional as Honey's.

"That was awesome," Lani commented as she clapped. "Other than the late canter-trot transition at B, they were practically perfect!"

"If you say so," Sam joked. "It just looked like a horse and rider going around in a bunch of circles to me. But they did it with class!"

Next it was Malory's turn. "Don't make any sudden loud noises," Lani quietly warned Sam. "Tybalt can be a little spooky."

Almost as if he'd heard her, the dark-bay gelding chose that moment to stop short and go bug-eyed at the pots of flowers decorating the entrance to the dressage ring. Malory stayed calm, soothing him with a few words before moving him on. Tybalt still kept one ear pricked towards the scary flowers, but he went where Malory pointed him.

Out of the corner of her eye, Lani saw Lynsey and Patience climbing into the stand. They were chatting and laughing with a couple of boys dressed in Saint Kit's colours.

Whew, I'm glad Lynsey didn't get here in time to see

Tybalt spook at those flowers, Lani thought. *She's already down on him since he didn't come from some fancy show yard. And now that Mal's been named captain of the Junior Jumping Team, Lynsey is out for blood.*

Tybalt had come to Chestnut Hill from a local dealer's yard less than a year earlier. He had started off as an anxious, spooky creature who could barely make it around the ring without a nervous breakdown. But gradually he'd turned into a pony who was athletic and rideable, though he could still be quite sensitive at times. That transformation was almost entirely thanks to Malory.

Lani had always admired her friend's gentle, patient way with horses. Malory hadn't grown up with a lot of the advantages that most of the girls at Chestnut Hill took for granted. She and her widowed father lived in a small apartment above his shoe store, and Malory had learned to ride at an inexpensive stable in nearby Cheney Falls. But that upbringing had served her well, winning her a prestigious riding scholarship to Chestnut Hill and also giving her the varied skills she'd needed to help Tybalt blossom.

As the bell rang to signal for Malory and Tybalt to begin, Lani crossed her fingers. Sam glanced down at her hand. He didn't say anything, but he crossed his fingers too. Lani smiled at him, then returned her attention to the ring.

Malory had Tybalt going in a swinging, forward trot as they came around the corner and entered at A. A couple of seventh-graders were posted just outside the dressage ring and were in charge of closing the gap when each pair entered. When they hurried forward Tybalt hesitated, flicking his ears back and raising his head as if trying to figure out what was going on behind him.

Malory pushed him on, not allowing him to lose focus. They executed a prompt, square halt at X, and Tybalt's ears swivelled forward again to focus on the judge as she nodded in response to Malory's salute.

Go, Mal! Lani thought as her friend trotted off again. Tybalt had a long, sweeping stride thanks to the thoroughbred part of his ancestry, and before long they were rounding the corner between C and M. There was another pot of flowers just outside the corner, and Tybalt bulged his inside shoulder and turned his head to stare. But it was only a momentary wobble. By the time they reached B, Malory had him in hand again, and the next time they passed one of the flowerpots, the bay gelding barely flicked an ear towards it.

"She's doing great!" Lani murmured to Sam, not taking her eyes off the pair. "She was worried about doing this event, since everything except the show-jumping is so new to him. But it looks like he's handling it fine so far."

Still, she hardly dared to breathe as she watched the pair perform. The same temperament that made Tybalt difficult also made him sensitive to his rider, which meant that Malory was able to time his transitions perfectly, barely needing to signal for canter or a circle before the gelding was doing it. Before long, Lani started to think they were going to give Honey and Minnie some serious competition!

Then, just as Tybalt was coming back to trot from his second canter circle, a car door slammed. The bay gelding jumped and bolted back into a ragged canter with his head straight up in the air and his eyes bulging with alarm.

"Easy, boy. Eeeeeasy," Malory said aloud, her words carrying across the stands, which had gone silent. Everyone seemed to be holding their breath as the pony scooted across the ring.

Lani winced, knowing that Malory would be penalized for using her voice. That was just like her, though. She cared a lot more about giving Tybalt a positive experience than she did about winning.

There was a long trot down the straight side after the canter circle, and Malory managed to calm Tybalt by the time they reached the next corner. As they rounded the curve, he was on the bit and clearly listening to his rider again, and Lani let out the breath she'd been holding.

"Well, *that* was interesting." Lynsey's sarcastic voice floated down the rail as Malory gave her final salute. "This year is going to be a disaster for the Junior Jumping Team if the team captain's horse is this unreliable."

She put extra emphasis on the words "team captain", and Lani rolled her eyes. "Get a life, Lynsey," she muttered, though she kept her voice quiet. She didn't want to give Lynsey the satisfaction of knowing she'd been bothered by the snarky comment.

"What was that all about?" Sam murmured, glancing towards Lynsey.

Lani shook her head. "Come on, let's go meet Mal

and see if she or Honey need any help," she said. "I'll explain then."

Sam took the coolbox back to his parents. Then he and Lani hurried towards the barn. "So what's the story?" he prompted as they walked. "That girl was Honey's roommate last year, right?"

"Lynsey Harrison," Lani confirmed with a nod. In seventh grade, Lynsey, Honey, and Dylan had shared a room. "She's a total snob, and thinks she should've been made captain of the junior jumping team just because she owns an expensive pony and competes on the A circuit."

"I see. But Malory made captain instead, and now she's holding a grudge?"

"Exactly."

Sam shrugged. "Well, Malory wouldn't have been made captain if she wasn't the best person for the job, right?" he said. "Lynsey will just have to get over it."

"Right," Lani agreed, biting her lip as they rounded the corner of the barn and came within sight of Malory and Tybalt. The bay gelding was already untacked, and Malory was easing a cooler over him.

She glanced up at Lani and Sam, her face looking pinched with stress. "Did you see that?"

"It wasn't that bad," Lani assured her loyally.

"Yeah," Sam joked. "If Lani hadn't told me, I would have thought it was all part of the test."

Lani laughed, guessing that Sam was trying to cheer Malory up. "Right," she said. "Spook at X, gallop at C, was it?"

Malory cracked a smile, but it didn't quite reach her eyes. "Something like that."

"Don't worry, Mal." Lani stepped forward and gave Tybalt a pat. "You handled it just fine. That's the important thing. It ended up being a good lesson and a positive experience for Tyb."

"Yeah, I know," Malory said, her expression still troubled as she gazed at the bay gelding. "I only wish we could learn those lessons *in* our lessons, instead of when the whole school's counting on us."

Chapter Three

"Need a leg up, Hernandez?" Dylan offered. "Or do you think you can get your legs to stop shaking long enough to mount on your own?"

Lani grimaced. "I think I can manage." Leading Colorado over to the mounting block, she checked her girth and then swung on.

"Stirrups feel OK?" Malory checked. "You sure you put them up enough after dressage?"

"I'm sure." Lani shot a mock kick at Honey, who had just hurried forward to give her boots a last-minute swipe with a clean rag. "And quit that, Honey! The beauty of cross-country is that it doesn't matter how we look."

"Right," Dylan said. "There's no judge to impress – just the clock and a bunch of solid jumps that won't fall down if you hit them. But no pressure."

Lani grinned at her. "Thanks, Walsh. I'll be sure to return that favour right before *you* head out there."

Soon she was riding Colorado up the hill behind the barn, heading across the grassy fields to the start of the cross-country course. The pony clearly knew this was no ordinary trail ride; his walk had an extra spring to it and his ears swivelled non-stop. He snorted and jumped when the breeze rattled the string that was marking out the course.

"Quit it, you goofball," Lani said with a laugh. "This is no time for you to start getting spooky, you hear me?"

The starting box was on a rise overlooking several of the jumps. The box consisted of a small corral-type enclosure a little bigger than a stall, open in front and on part of one side, constructed of white plastic pipe. Lani was happy to see Ms Carmichael standing just outside it. She also spotted her friends racing up the hill on foot to one of the spectator areas nearby. When the course had been designed, one of the things Ms Carmichael had requested was for it to be as viewer-friendly as possible. Aside from a couple of jumps in the woods, all of the course was visible from the main spectator area.

"Ready to go, Lani?" the riding director asked as Lani rode up.

"Ready as I'll ever be." Lani gave Colorado a pat on the neck. "But don't worry. Even if I forget what to do, Colorado will save us. He was born for cross-country!"

"Don't get overly confident," Ms Carmichael warned. "I know Colorado enjoyed cross-country jumping in our lessons. But this is different – he'll be out there all on his own, without his herdmates nearby to give him confidence. Besides, as I'm always telling you, horses pick up on our feelings. If you're nervous because it's show day, he'll feel it and wonder if he should be nervous too. That could lead to a stop or run-out if you're not on your toes."

"On my toes?" Lani wriggled her feet in the stirrups. "But wait, you're always telling us to put our heels down ... Have I been going about this riding thing all wrong this whole time?"

Ms Carmichael rolled her eyes. But Lani was pretty sure she spotted a twinkle in them. "All right, they're going to count you down now. Good luck, Lani."

"Thanks."

Lani urged Colorado through one of the openings into the start box. Chloe Bates, a senior from Granville dorm, was acting as the official starter. She held up her stopwatch.

"Ten seconds, Lani," she said. "Nine, eight, seven..."

Lani closed her eyes briefly, psyching herself up just as she did when she was on deck in a softball game. She felt Colorado's muscles tense beneath her and wondered if he knew what was coming.

Chloe was still counting, "...three, two, one – go! Good luck, Lani!"

"Thanks!" Lani shouted as she and Colorado burst into motion, first at a brisk trot and then, within a few strides, a canter. She fixed her gaze on the first jump, an inviting log decorated with pumpkins. "Here we go, boy!" she cried.

"Wow, that was fun!" Lani exclaimed as she pulled off Colorado's saddle and rested it on his door. "But Ms Carmichael was right – it was *definitely* different from when we did those jumps in lessons." She groaned and rubbed her legs. "Colorado really made me work for a few of the spookier jumps."

Dylan bustled into the stall with a bucket and started sponging the dun pony's saddle mark. "Really? But Colorado isn't spooky."

"Still, this was his first time out there all alone." Malory glanced up from unfastening Colorado's jumping boots. "Even the most honest horse can get worried about something new."

Lani nodded. She was glad Ms Carmichael had reminded her of that before she'd started. She'd still been surprised when Colorado had hung back approaching the ditch on course. He'd jumped it several times over the past week with no hesitation at all. But Lani realized it probably looked a lot scarier to him now that it was marked off with hay bales at either end. Luckily he'd gone ahead and jumped it after she'd given him a few kicks and a whap behind the saddle with her crop. By the end, both her arms and her legs were sore but she was grinning – they'd ridden clear and well within the time allowed.

"Where's Honey?" she asked her friends. "Is she warming up already?"

"Uh huh." Malory straightened up and dropped the boots in the aisle outside Colorado's stall. "Her parents and Sam already headed up the hill to watch. Want to run up there and join them? You should be able to make it in time for her round if Dylan and I finish with Colorado."

"Are you sure you don't mind?"

"We're sure." Malory glanced over at Dylan, who nodded. "We're stuck down here anyway, since we need to change back into our show clothes and get our ponies tacked up again soon."

"You'll have to cheer Honey on for all three of us," Dylan added.

"Will do," Lani promised. "Thanks, guys. You're the best!"

She ran all the way up to the viewing area, still pumped up by her clean round. Now that it was over, she felt a lot more relaxed about the rest of the competition. All that was left was show-jumping, although Lani knew she'd have her work cut out if she wanted Colorado to stay balanced and collected over fences in the ring after their exhilarating gallop.

Sam and his parents had spread a picnic blanket on the grass in a shady spot beneath the branches of a large oak tree.

"Congratulations, Lani," Mrs Harper said with a smile. "You looked quite professional out there."

"Thanks. I couldn't have done it without such a great pony," Lani said, flopping down on the picnic blanket beside Sam.

"I shouldn't think so," Sam said. "You'd look awfully funny running around out there jumping over logs and things on your own two feet. Plus I seriously doubt you'd make the time."

"Ha, ha!" Lani said, sticking out her tongue at him as his parents chuckled. "I didn't miss Honey's round, did I?"

"No, Lani." Mr Harper checked his watch. "Her start time is in about ten minutes."

"The countdown begins!" Sam said, raising his muffin in a mock salute.

"Careful, Sam," his mother chided gently. "You're dropping crumbs everywhere. Before long we'll all be carried off by ants!" She brushed at a tiny insect crawling around on the blanket.

Lani flicked a muffin crumb from near her foot, then laughed as two ants appeared and scurried toward it from opposite directions. "Check it out," she said. "Those two ants both have their eyes on the prize."

"Cool," Sam said. "Ant races!"

Lani leaned forward to study the tiny insects. "Maybe we could start a new sport – ant eventing."

"It would be a hit!" Sam exclaimed. "I mean, who could resist watching a bunch of ants in cute little dressage jackets and boots?"

Lani nodded with mock seriousness. "To be followed, of course, by the adrenalin-pumped excitement of ant cross-country."

"And the best part is, you wouldn't need a huge field to hold it in." Sam waved a hand to indicate the course surrounding them. "You could do it in a shoebox!"

Lani laughed. "True," she said. "And the jumps wouldn't take months to build, either, like with our course. All you'd have to do is stack a couple of matchsticks, and *voilà*! Log-pile jump!"

Sam snapped his fingers. "It's brilliant, I tell you,

brilliant! We should be writing this down – it's bound to be the next great Olympic sport!"

"Totally!" Lani was laughing harder by now. "But what about show-jumping? It's going to be tough to find jump cups that small…"

For the next few minutes the two of them were so busy planning their new sport – and laughing like hyenas at their ideas – that Mr Harper had to tell them twice before they realized that Honey and Minnie were approaching the starting box. Lani sat back, still smiling as she watched her friend circle the mare around the box waiting for her turn to go in. Ms Carmichael was still there, and though they were too far away to hear what she was saying, Honey was nodding.

Beside her, Lani was aware of Sam sitting up straight and watching his sister. *I'd almost forgotten how goofy Sam's sense of humour is*, she thought. *I guess that's why we get along so well – he's almost as goofy as I am!*

A moment later Honey rode into the starting box, and Lani forgot about everything else. She held her breath as the sound of the starter's countdown drifted towards them.

"And they're off!" she cried as Minnie trotted out of the box, then picked up an easy canter, her dainty ears pricked towards the first jump. "Just ride her forward, Honey…"

From their vantage spot, Lani and the others were able to see almost all the jumps on the course. Minnie cleared most of them easily out of stride. The only exception was the ditch. Even from a dozen strides away, Lani could tell that the pretty grey mare was looking hard at the strange obstacle up ahead.

"Push her, Honey," she chanted, even though there was no way her friend could hear her from that distance. "Leg on. More leg. Leg ... Aw, rats!" she exclaimed as Minnie slid to a stop a stride out, lowering her head and snorting at the ditch before backing up a few steps.

"Oh, dear," Mrs Harper said. "Well, at least she stayed on!"

"Bummer." Lani sighed, disappointed on her friend's behalf. "They were working on a clean round up until then."

Honey turned Minnie away, circling her and coming at the ditch again. This time Lani could see her friend sit back and drive the pony on for the last several strides. Minnie still looked a bit reluctant, but she popped over the ditch with plenty of room to spare. After that, she gave Honey no more trouble, and the pair finished with just twenty penalty points for the single refusal.

"Ugh," Dylan moaned as she buttoned the collar of her shirt. "I still can't believe I got two time faults on cross-country!"

"Yeah." Lani looked up from buckling Colorado's throatlatch and grinned. "Leave it to you and Morello to come in five whole seconds *under* the speed fault time!"

The four friends were in the barn dissecting their performances as they prepared for the final element of the day's event, show-jumping. Lani chuckled as she thought back over Dylan's cross-country course. Morello hadn't given Dylan any trouble at any of the jumps, even the dreaded ditch. However, he'd been so excited about being out on the course that he'd galloped his heart out between fences, and Dylan hadn't had much luck slowing him down.

"Never mind, Dylan," Malory said. "You were clear other than that – that's awesome."

Lani shot a sympathetic look at Malory, who was easing Tybalt's girth up another hole as he stood in the cross-ties. She'd seen her cross-country round, too. Unfortunately, it hadn't gone as well for Malory as it had for the rest of them. It had been obvious from the start that Tybalt was unsettled by the crowds and didn't like being out in the open on his own. He'd tried to sidle out of the starting box as soon as Malory rode him in, then after the countdown he'd burst out at a full gallop with his head straight up in the air. Malory had eased him down to a canter by the time they'd reached the first jump, but after getting a look at the pumpkin decorations, Tybalt had hesitated, then popped the jump from a near standstill, just about unseating the normally Velcro-butted Malory. They'd managed the next few jumps, though they weren't much prettier. But the palisade jump, which was decorated with garlands of autumn leaves and a stuffed squirrel, had completely blown the skittish gelding's mind. Despite Malory's best efforts, he'd skidded to a stop in front of it three times in a row, earning him elimination from the competition.

"You did a fantastic job getting Tybalt around the first part of the course, Malory," Honey said loyally.

"Definitely," Lani agreed. "I'm sure nobody else could've got him anywhere near some of those jumps."

"Thanks." Malory smiled ruefully. "I figured it was worth a try, even though I always knew Tybalt didn't have a cross-country kind of temperament. All things considered, I think we did OK. And Ms Carmichael said that since this is just a schooling event, I can still take him in for the show-jumping. We think it will help restore his confidence to end the day with something familiar."

"Well, I certainly hope so!" Lynsey said loudly. She had just appeared in the aisle and was gazing at them with disdain. "We wouldn't want the team captain's horse to be spooky and unpredictable, would we?" Her voice dripped with sarcasm.

"Stuff it, Lynsey," Dylan said, clearly in no mood for more creative insults. "And by the way, didn't your mother ever teach you not to butt in on private conversations?"

"Oh, was it meant to be private?" Lynsey put her hands on her hips and snorted. "Because they can probably hear your foghorn of a voice on the moon, Dylan." With a toss of her head, she pranced towards her pony's stall.

"Whatever," Lani said, frowning after her. "Don't pay any attention to her, Mal. We all know Tybalt's a star – and so are you."

Malory and Tybalt went on to prove that – sort of,

anyway – during their show-jumping round. Malory played it safe, riding the course like a hunter class. Tybalt had a long stride and plenty of speed, so there was no need for them to hurry to make the time. The plan paid off. Tybalt came into the ring high-headed and anxious-looking, but he visibly relaxed after the first couple of jumps. Malory ended up very pleased with him despite an unlucky rail in the second part of the combination that gave them four faults.

Meanwhile, Lani found that Colorado hadn't calmed down from his exciting cross-country round. She could tell he was still hyped up as soon as she swung her leg over, but she managed to keep his enthusiasm under control until they reached the big, airy oxer near the end of the course. As soon as they came out of the corner, she felt his stride flatten out and did her best to reel him in. But it was no good. He flung himself at the jump, bringing the front rail down with his forelegs and, for good measure, the back rail with his hinds. Lani winced as she heard the clatter. But she stayed as focused as she could, half-halting strongly enough to settle him for the last two jumps.

Honey didn't make any obvious mistakes taking Minnie around the course, but the pony still knocked down two rails. Afterwards, Honey shrugged off her disappointment; she thought Minnie was just a little tired from the long day. Out of the four of them, only Dylan managed a clear round. Morello tapped the wall with his hind legs, but the blocks stayed in place.

Later, a few minutes after the last of the Senior

riders had finished their rounds, Lani found her friends gathered near the ring. Most of the other riders from the various schools were also milling around after returning their horses to the trailers.

"Did they announce the placings yet?" Lani gasped. She'd just taken Colorado to his turnout paddock, which meant she'd been out of hearing range of the PA system.

Dylan shook her head. "Nope, and for once I have no guesses about who won," she admitted. "With thirty riders in our section and three phases with all the confusing scoring, it's way too hard to keep track."

"I know what you mean," Malory said. "Even the dressage is opposite from the way we're used to – instead of wanting the highest score like in regular dressage shows, in eventing they reverse things so you want the lowest score."

Honey was the only one of the four who had some prior eventing experience. "It does seem rather complex at first," she agreed. "But you get used to it." She shrugged. "Still, I haven't the foggiest clue how any of us did either."

Ms Carmichael hurried past just in time to hear her, a sheaf of papers clutched in one hand. "Stay tuned, then," she told the girls. "I'm about to announce the results."

"Can't we get a sneak preview?" Lani begged. "Pretty please?"

The riding director smiled sympathetically. "Sorry, that wouldn't be fair."

She hurried off in the direction of the announcer's

stand. Dylan stared after her. "Hmm," she said. "Aunt Ali looked pretty cheerful. Maybe that means Chestnut Hill kicked butt and swept the ribbons!"

Lani laughed. Ms Carmichael was Dylan's aunt, which did give Dylan some extra insight at times. But this time, she suspected her friend's prediction might be mostly wishful thinking.

"I don't know," she said. "Some of the teams from the other schools looked pretty strong. I heard that one girl from Allbright's has evented up to Prelim level. I'll be happy as long as Colorado and I didn't come in last. That would be so embarrassing!"

As it turned out, none of them needed to be embarrassed. When Ms Carmichael announced the placings, it turned out that the girl Lani had mentioned, Alison Hobart, had come in first in the Junior Open section. Boys from Saint Kit's had placed second and third, and Dylan and Morello were fourth.

"What?" Dylan exclaimed when Ms Carmichael announced her name. "But we had those time penalties!"

Lani pounded her on the back, grinning. "Yeah, but you had an awesome dressage score," she reminded her. "Not to mention the clean round in show-jumping. Face it, Walsh – you rocked it!"

Ms Carmichael went on to read out the rest of the placings. Honey and Minnie had finished ninth, with their strong dressage score making up for the penalties in the other two rounds. Lani and Colorado were twelfth.

"Hey, it's not last, right?" Lani joked, grinning. She always tried her best to win in any sport, but she also knew that when it came to riding, it wasn't always about the red ribbons. And she was pleased with her twelfth-place finish – after all, who would have thought that a Colorado cowgirl and a former ranch pony could even complete a three-phase event, let alone place in the top half of their class?

"Ooh, look – there's Caleb." Dylan poked Malory in the arm. "Shouldn't we go over and say hello?"

Caleb Smith was a ninth-grader at Saint Kit's, but Malory had first met him through her local riding stable in Cheney Falls. The two of them had had their ups and down over the past year, but they had mostly worked out their problems recently and were now a couple again.

Without waiting for an answer, Dylan grabbed Malory and started dragging her off toward a small cluster of Saint Kit's riders nearby. Honey smiled and followed.

"I'll be right there," Lani called after the others. "I want to say hi to Alison from Allbright's. She loaned me her spare crop so I need to give it back."

As she headed back to her friends after speaking to Alison, she saw Sam weaving through the crowd towards her.

"Congratulations," he said, his cheeks so pink that Lani wondered if the long day had been too much for him. As healthy as he looked, it was easy to forget he'd been so sick not long ago. "You did great."

"Thanks. And how about that Honey, huh?" Lani said. "She and Minnie were superstars!"

"Uh huh. I need to go find her, and Dylan and Malory, too. But first…" Sam took a deep breath. "Um, listen. My dad got three tickets to a baseball match next Saturday – a local minor-league team's playoffs, I think – but Mum's been invited to lunch by a neighbour. I know it's short notice and you might be busy or whatever, but I was just wondering – would you like to go with us?"

He finished up the last part all in a rush, his face looking redder than ever. Lani grinned.

"First of all, it's a baseball *game*, not a match," she said. "And secondly, I'd love to go! For one thing, I can't stand the thought of you and your dad embarrassing yourselves by wandering around a public game calling it a match and looking for tea and stuff."

Sam burst out laughing, his pink cheeks fading a bit until his face was closer to its normal colour. "Brilliant!" he said. "Er, that is, I mean – awesome! There, is that American enough for you?"

"Totally," Lani assured him. "And we're going to have an absolutely *brilliant* time at that match!"

Chapter Four

"Lani has a da-a-ate! Lani has a da-a-ate!" Dylan sang as the four friends walked through the corridors of Adams dorm that evening.

Lani rolled her eyes. "Please," she said, trying to sound blasé. "I keep telling you, it's not a date. It's just a ball game."

"Right." Malory grinned. "A ball game that you're going to with a certain very cute boy!"

"Wait, are you saying you think my dad is cute, Mal?" Honey joked. "Mum will be jealous!"

"You guys are obsessed with romance." Lani rolled her eyes again. "If you don't knock it off, I might have to forbid Honey and Malory from seeing Josh and Caleb for the rest of the term – it's obviously going to their heads."

"Horrors!" Dylan placed a hand over her heart, almost knocking off her green fourth-place rosette, which she'd been wearing on her shirt since the event had ended several hours earlier. "You can't do that, Lani. What would we have to tease them about then?"

"Hmm." Lani put a finger to her chin, pretending to ponder what Dylan had said. "Good point. I guess I can let it slide this time."

They'd reached the Junior Common Room. It was crowded with Adams students relaxing after dinner. A group of seventh-graders had staked out the TV to play *Dance Dance Revolution*, while a handful of eighth-graders were poring over some magazines on the couch near the windows.

Lynsey was perched on a chair painting her toenails a shocking shade of magenta. "Are you planning to wear that thing all weekend?" she asked, using her nail-polish wand to point at the rosette flapping from Dylan's shirt. "Pretty pathetic fashion statement, Dylan – even for you."

"Not just all weekend," Dylan replied, straight-faced. "I thought I'd wear it for the rest of the year. Maybe next year, too."

Lynsey rolled her eyes and capped her nail polish, stretching her leg out to admire her toes. "That little joke might actually be funny if your entire wardrobe wasn't a huge fashion violation. My clothes are embarrassed to be stuck in the same room as yours."

"Don't be a hater just 'cause you're jealous, Lynsey," Dylan retorted. "If you keep trying, maybe someday you'll dress as well as me. Probably not, but you never know."

Lynsey just snorted at that. "Whatever, Dylan."

"Seriously, though," Dylan said to her friends as they wandered past Lynsey into the middle of the room,

"I'm not only wearing this rosette to irritate Lynsey, though that's a huge bonus. Finishing so well today just confirmed that I made the right decision in deciding to keep working with Morello instead of letting my parents buy me that expensive show pony."

Honey smiled. "For the record, I think you made the right decision, too," she said.

Lani had thought that Lynsey was out of earshot, but she was wrong. "Are you serious, Dylan?" Lynsey exclaimed. "I still can't believe you turned down the chance to buy Starlight Express. Blue and I competed against him last summer, and he's a top-flight horse." She rolled her eyes. "I mean, that skewbald thing you ride might do OK galloping around and flinging himself over logs and stuff, but he's not a proper show pony, and you know it."

"Ignore her," Honey murmured as Lynsey turned and stalked off. "She's just obsessed with winning."

Malory frowned. "I know she's used to winning everything, but that doesn't give her the right to talk to Dylan like that."

Lani shrugged. "Since when do any of us pay attention to Lynsey, anyway?"

"Good point," Dylan agreed. "Come on, let's chase the seventh-graders away from the video game. It's our turn!"

Over the course of the next week, Lani found it harder and harder to focus in her classes. On Tuesday, when her geography teacher compared the topography of England

44

to that of France, Lani ended up drifting off into her own comparison of the English landscapes she'd heard about from Sam and Honey to those of the United States. On Thursday, when Mme Dubois gave a lecture on tricky vocabulary terms, Lani hardly heard it because she was too busy making a mental list of interesting baseball terms she could teach Sam. And on Friday, she found herself zoning out in her favourite class, science, because she was busy trying to figure out what to wear to the game the next day.

Wow, she thought ruefully as she tuned back in just in time to scribble down the details of the test Mrs Marshall had announced for the following week. *Since when do I spend more than two seconds deciding what to wear?*

That evening as she got ready for bed, she glanced over at Honey, who was reading a horse magazine in the bed across from her. Normally Lani would ask her roommate for fashion advice. Honey might not be as couture-conscious as Dylan, but she had a natural flair for fashion that Lani admired.

But for some reason it felt funny asking Honey for advice this time. Lani stared at her friend, perplexed. Was it because she was going to the game with Sam, and Sam was Honey's twin brother?

Maybe, she admitted to herself. *I mean, Honey obviously knows that I'm going to the game with Sam and their dad. But does she know I might possibly have the teeniest, tiniest little bit of a crush on Sam, and that's why I'm looking forward to it so much?* She grimaced at the thought. *I hope not, because it's totally lame to start going all gooey over him just because he asked me to the game. I mean, who else is he going to ask? He's been sick since he moved to this country and barely knows anyone else, let alone anyone else who likes baseball…*

Just then, Honey looked up. "What's the matter?" she asked, lowering her magazine. "You look rather funny."

"Sorry." Lani laughed self-consciously. "Just tired, I guess."

Normally she could talk to Honey about anything. But this was different. *Besides, there's nothing to talk about – to Honey or anyone else*, she told herself firmly. *It's just two friends going to a game. End of story*.

"They're here!" Honey called from the window of the dorm room.

Lani looked up from tying the laces of her Nikes. "What?"

"Dad and Sam." Honey gestured towards the window. "I just saw the car pull up out front."

"Oh." Lani stood up, resisting the urge to glance at her reflection in the mirror over the dresser. After spending the past two days debating what to wear, she'd finally settled on her favourite worn-in pair of Levis and a Colorado Rockies T-shirt. "Um, guess I'd better get out there."

Honey smiled. "Have fun at the game."

"Thanks." Lani hesitated, feeling guilty and a little nervous, though she wasn't sure why. "Um, why don't you come with us?" she blurted out.

46

Honey blinked in surprise. "What?"

Lani shrugged. "If I'm going to teach half your family about baseball, why not go for three-quarters?" she said. "Come on, it could be fun! I'm sure there are still tickets available – it's not like the Mid-County Rebels are likely to sell out the stadium even if it is the playoffs. The Senior softball team could probably give them a run for their money."

"Well, you do make it sound tempting," Honey said. "But I'll pass. Dylan and Malory and I decided to go to the mall this afternoon, remember?"

"Oh. OK." Lani glanced towards the window. "Um, guess I'd better go. Have fun today."

"You too."

"Thank goodness we're here. I'm not sure I could take any more of the baseball lecture. Or Lani's singing."

Lani glanced at Mr Harper, pretty sure he was joking. She'd just finished teaching Sam the lyrics to "Take Me Out to the Ball Game".

"Hey, there's plenty more I could teach you," she joked back. "I haven't even started on the designated-hitter rule or the importance of the earned run average."

In the front passenger seat, Sam was already unbuckling his seatbelt. "Enough statistics and songs," he said. "Time for a practical lesson."

Lani grinned. During the half-hour drive, she and Sam had chattered non-stop. After about three minutes, Lani had wondered why she'd been nervous at all. Sam was super easy to talk to, and interested in learning everything she could teach him about baseball. And thanks to growing up a tomboy with a sports-crazy father who'd always hoped for a son but ended up with four daughters, Lani could teach him quite a bit.

She climbed out of the car and stretched. It was a gorgeous fall day. The leaves were just starting to turn, and the weather was warm and sunny with only the slightest nip in the breeze hinting at winter's approach. The game was taking place at a small stadium shared with local university teams. The car park was already full. Several people were setting out picnic lunches on the tailgates of their cars. Some had brought portable grills, and the scents of sizzling burgers and hot dogs added to the lively scene.

"Come on." Lani realized it had been a long time since she'd been to a baseball game. "Let's get in there and root, root, root for the home team!"

Soon they were inside climbing the metal stands towards their seats, which were about halfway up the first section. Lani charged ahead, eager to get settled in for the game.

"Hang on, Lani!" Mr Harper called. "Slow down a bit, can you? We don't want Sam getting winded."

"I'm all right, Dad." Sam pushed past his father and hurried up the steps two at a time to catch up with Lani. She noticed that he did sound a little out of breath, though his voice was strong as he called back down to his father. "I'm not winded at all, see?"

Mr Harper looked worried as he climbed up after

him. "All right. But take it easy, OK? The game hasn't even started yet – there's no hurry."

When they found their seats, Sam took the one in the middle, with his father on his left and Lani on his right on the aisle.

"Hey, these are pretty good seats," Lani said, surveying the view. They were sitting almost directly at the centre field. Because it was a relatively small park, that gave them a good view of the entire diamond. "Who'd you have to bribe to get them, Mr H?"

Sam's father didn't seem to have heard her. He was digging into the tote bag he'd brought in. "Here you go, Sam," he said, pulling out a chair cushion. "Sit on this. These metal seats are pretty hard. Would you like one too, Lani? I brought an extra."

"No, thanks," Lani said with a grin, propping her feet on the empty seat in front of her. "It wouldn't be a real game if my butt wasn't sore at the end of it."

Sam laughed, then pushed away the cushion. "I want to get the whole American baseball experience," he told his father. "Sore behind and all."

"Are you sure?" Mr Harper nudged at him with the corner of the cushion. "But you're still so thin, and your seatbones…"

"My seatbones will be fine," Sam said with an edge of irritation in his voice. "Thanks all the same, Dad. Really."

For a moment Mr Harper looked ready to argue. But instead he shrugged and stuck the cushion back in the bag.

I guess it's not easy for him to relax, Lani thought. *Sam was sick for so long, and for a while it looked like they might lose him ... I suppose it's no wonder if his parents are still kind of tense.*

She forgot about that as soon as the game started. The crowd roared as the home team took the field, and Lani and Sam joined in with enthusiasm. And when the Rebels scored the first run of the game, Sam was on his feet pumping his fist even before Lani was.

As they both sat back down again, Lani glanced over to see if Mr Harper was enjoying the game as much as his son. She found him gazing at Sam with a troubled look on his face. Lani wondered if he was paying attention to the action on the field at all.

"Hey, you guys, what's a baseball game without some greasy food?" she said, rubbing her stomach. "I think I saw a hot-dog stand down by the entrance where we came in. Want me to grab us some chilli dogs?"

"Sounds great!" Sam said immediately. "I'll come with you."

"I have a better idea." Mr Harper put a hand on Sam's shoulder before he could stand up. "Why don't I fetch the snacks? It's so crowded, I'm sure it'll be a struggle for you kids to get down there and back." He climbed to his feet and stepped past them before they could protest. Out in the aisle, he paused and glanced back at Sam. "Son, just sit down if you're feeling at all tired, all right?"

"Sure, Dad." As soon as his father had hurried down the steps and disappeared out of sight, Sam turned to

Lani and sighed. "Sorry about my dad," he said. "I'm afraid he's still rather overprotective."

"No need to apologize," Lani replied. "I'm sure it's just taking your family a while to get used to the idea that you're better, that's all. Totally understandable." She grinned. "And hey – this way your dad has to pay for the hot dogs!"

Sam grinned back. "True enough. Though I'm hoping you're not too hungry, because I'm so famished I might have to eat all the hot dogs myself."

"Fat chance, buddy," Lani joked in return. "You'll have to fight me for them!"

"No way, I've got to make up for lost time," Sam retorted, his eyes sparkling. "You wouldn't deprive a poor cancer survivor of his life-sustaining food, would you?"

Lani laughed. "Just watch me!" She was glad – and impressed – to see that Sam had a sense of humour about his recent health crisis. "Besides, since when are you so hungry? The hot dogs were *my* idea, remember?"

"I know." Sam smiled at her. "And I'm sure you come up with all the best ideas, Lani."

Lani gulped. "Um, that's true," she said, going for the same light, joking tone despite the way he was looking straight at her. She stared back for a long moment, not knowing what else to say. Feeling self-conscious, she glanced at the field. "Hey, check it out," she said. "Looks like they're changing pitchers."

She could tell her face was going pink as she looked back at Sam and found him still staring at her. She wondered if he'd even heard what she'd just said.

OK, this is bizarre, she said. *A second ago we were just hanging out, watching some baseball and joking around about hot dogs. And now everything has gone weird and I have no idea what we're talking about...*

"Home run!" someone shrieked from the row of seats behind them. There was a general roar, and suddenly the entire stadium was on its feet.

Sam and Lani both looked up. "Hey, here comes the ball!" Lani cried, seeing the baseball spinning straight towards their section of the stands. She jumped to her feet.

Beside her, Sam did the same. He stretched out both hands and the ball whizzed towards them. "I'll get it!"

"No way, it's mine!" Lani said, playfully elbowing him aside.

"Out of my way, girl!" Sam pushed back against her. They jostled and shoved at each other for a moment, both of them laughing.

Then the ball was upon them. Lani squinted at it and leaped up – just in time to grab it out of the air.

Chapter Five

"Got it!" Lani crowed, holding the ball up over her head and doing a victory jig. Other spectators nearby laughed and clapped.

"Way to go, Lani!" Sam said with a grin. "Too bad you had to practically bowl me over."

Lani stuck out her tongue at him. "Like my dad always says, if you can't run with the big dogs, stay on the porch."

She was still grinning when she noticed Mr Harper hurrying towards them, pushing his way through the crowd with a rather grim expression on his face and a tray of hot dogs and sodas in his hands. With a gulp, Lani wondered if he'd seen her push Sam aside to grab the ball.

Considering how protective Sam's dad has been acting today, he'll probably have me arrested for assault and battery, she thought ruefully. It had felt perfectly natural to roughhouse with Sam the same way she would with anyone, especially after that weird moment they'd just had. But had it been too much too soon?

When she glanced at Sam, she was relieved to see that he looked fine. He even turned and traded a high five with the college-aged boy behind them as the home run score was announced.

"Looks like I missed some excitement," Mr Harper said as he reached their row. "Everyone all right?"

"Check it out, Dad!" Sam exclaimed. "Lani caught the home run ball! Isn't that cool?"

"Yes, I suppose so." Mr Harper set down the tray of food on his seat. His words were slower and more measured as he turned to her. "Lani, I do understand the excitement of the game. But I hope you can remember that Sam isn't back to his full strength yet. We have to keep that in mind, all right?"

"Sure, Mr Harper," Lani said, feeling herself go red. She could tell that he was upset but trying to hide it. "Sorry."

Meanwhile Sam's gleeful expression had changed to one of irritation. "She didn't do anything wrong, Dad," he said. "She just didn't treat me like I'm made of glass, that's all."

Lani bit her lip. She couldn't help agreeing with Sam that his father was overreacting. Still, she felt guilty for causing them to argue, even though she hadn't meant to do it.

"I think we'd better eat our hot dogs and then call it a day," Mr Harper's voice was firm. "We've still got the long drive home, after all."

"No way, Dad! It's only the third inning." Sam glanced at Lani, clearly expecting her to back him up.

But Lani shrugged. "It's OK," she said meekly, not wanting to cause any further friction between Sam and his dad. "He's right. It is a long drive, and I have a lot of homework this weekend."

They were almost back to Chestnut Hill when Lani picked up the home run ball she'd caught and tossed it between the two front seats on to Sam's lap. "Hey," she said. "Why don't you keep this? You know – as a souvenir of your first all-American baseball game."

"What?" Sam turned the ball over in his hands, glancing back at her. "Don't be crazy, Lani. You caught it – it's yours by rights."

"I know. But I want you to have it." Lani shrugged. "Anyway, I already have a lucky baseball. My grandpa gave it to me when he died. So I don't need another one."

Sam stared down at the ball in his hands. Lani couldn't see his face clearly from the back seat, but she thought he looked almost angry.

"What's the matter?" she asked. "Don't you want it?"

"Nothing. I mean, sure." Sam still didn't meet her eye. "Uh, thanks."

Lani felt a flash of annoyance. Despite their abrupt departure from the game, the car ride home had been pleasant so far. Even Mr Harper had been especially quick to chuckle or toss in a joke, as if trying to make up for his strict behaviour earlier. So why had her offer of the game ball suddenly turned things sour?

Whatever his problem was, she wasn't about to let him get away with it. The day had been too much fun so far to let it end on a bad note.

"Besides," she said, careful to keep her tone light, "you need a ball to practise with if I'm going to teach you how to play. Batting is one thing, but if you're ever going to have a prayer of learning to pitch, it's going to take some work."

Sam shot her a look, then broke into a smile. "Really?" he said. "You think you can teach me how to play baseball?"

"Sure, why not?" Lani noticed Mr Harper shooting Sam a disapproving look, but she ignored it. "I'm a great coach, if I do say so myself. If we get started now, you'll probably be ready for the professional league by spring training."

"Cool! We'll have to figure out a time to get started." Whatever had been bothering Sam a moment ago, it seemed to be forgotten. "What do you say, Dad? Maybe we could drive over next weekend."

"We'll have to see." Mr Harper kept his eyes on the road as he hit the indicator for the turn into Chestnut Hill's long, sweeping drive. "It's a busy time of year. We might not be able to make it over here again anytime soon."

Sam shrugged, then twisted around again to face Lani. "Maybe we can keep in touch by email and figure out a time."

"That sounds good. Here, I'll write down my email address." Lani knew she could just get Sam's address from Honey, but somehow that seemed too complicated. She scribbled her name and address on a scrap of paper and handed it to him, feeling tingly all of a sudden. Was seeing Sam on the weekends going to become a regular thing? She had to admit she wouldn't mind that at all.

She was still tingling when she pushed open the door of her dorm room a few minutes later. Honey was flopped on her stomach on her bed reading her history textbook. She looked up with a smile when Lani came in.

"You're back!" she said. "How was the game?"

"Good. We didn't stick around for the whole thing, but the Rebels were up by three when we left."

Honey looked puzzled. "You mean you left early? How come? Did Sam get tired?"

Lani bent down to pull off her shoes, using it as an excuse not to answer for a second. If she had been with anyone else that day, she would have poured out the whole story to Honey then and there – Mr Harper's overprotectiveness, the incident with the home run ball, her feelings later in the car … But somehow it didn't feel right.

"Nah, you know how it is," she said breezily, turning away from Honey as she tossed her shoes into her wardrobe. "We just didn't want to hang around there all day. Listen, I want to run down to the barn and see Colorado before dinner. I'll be back in a while, OK?"

"OK. Don't be too late – there's lasagne tonight, and you know how fast it always goes." Honey returned her attention to her book.

Lani slipped on her paddock boots and hurried out into the hall without even tying the laces. For a second she almost turned back and spilled everything to her friend after all, but in the end she kept walking. Normally she could talk to Honey about anything, and she wasn't sure why this should be any different just because Sam was Honey's brother. But somehow, it was.

"All right, that should do it." Ms Carmichael stepped back from the grid she'd set up in the indoor arena. "Now, the purpose of this exercise is to get the ponies thinking and balanced again. After racing around the cross-country course last weekend and then taking this past week off from jumping, we want to remind them how to sit back on their hocks and jump up and over vertical fences again."

"Great," Lynsey muttered from her spot between Lani and Tessa Harding. "Figures we'd need some remedial jumping classes after that mess last week. Too bad for those of us who don't need it."

Lani glanced over at Dylan on her other side just long enough for both of them to roll their eyes. Then she returned her gaze to the grid. As usual, Lynsey's snide remarks weren't worth much attention.

"Looks like fun, doesn't it, Colorado?" she murmured, giving her pony a pat. The gymnastic exercise consisted of four trot poles leading to a crossrail, followed by one stride to an oxer and another single stride to a vertical.

Lynsey shot her a scornful look. "Right, fun," she said.

"Let's hope he doesn't have a cross-country flashback and send rails flying like he did in your show-jumping round." She shook her head. "It's a well-known fact that some ponies just don't have the mind or the breeding for proper jumping."

"All right, who wants to go first?" Ms Carmichael invited. "Lynsey, you seem to be in a chatty mood today. Does that mean you're volunteering?"

Lynsey shrugged and gathered up her reins. "Sure, why not?" she said. "Although Blue doesn't really need reminding how to jump properly, of course."

She nudged her pony into a trot, making a neat circle before entering the grid. She and Bluegrass swept through flawlessly, the roan pony's neat hooves landing like clockwork between the trot poles and his forelegs tucking neatly over each of the jumping elements.

"Nicely done," Ms Carmichael said when she pulled up. "Lani, you're next."

"Come on, boy," Lani said. "Let's see what we can do."

She asked for a trot and made a circle just as Lynsey had done. Colorado trotted calmly until he got a look at the grid. Then his ears pricked and he surged forward, almost breaking into a canter. Lani half-halted just in time, but he was still moving too fast as they reached the trot poles and the pony ended up hitting the last two with a thunk. He lunged over the crossrail, landing at a flattened-out canter that put him far too close to the oxer. He did his best to clear it anyway, twisting in the air, but the rails clattered to the ground behind him. The single stride between the oxer and vertical was awkward and choppy, and he barely managed to get over the vertical without bringing it down, too.

"Oops," Lani said, bringing him around in a rushed circle before managing to slow him back to a trot. "That wasn't pretty."

"No kidding," Lynsey said sourly. "And you all wondered why I wouldn't let Blue go galumphing around a cross-country course?" She nodded towards the fallen poles, which Ms Carmichael was resetting. "*That's* why."

"Oh, come on, Lynsey," Jo-Ann Swelby said with a laugh. "I think you're just jealous 'cause we all had fun out there last Saturday and you missed it." She grinned and patted Quest, the dapple-grey gelding she was riding that day, who had also been her partner in the event. "Isn't that right, boy?"

Lynsey rolled her eyes. "As if."

"Never mind, Lani," Honey added as Lani rode by, working hard at getting Colorado on the aids and listening. "Colorado was such a star on cross-country that he's excited, that's all."

"She's right," Ms Carmichael put in. "Try it again, Lani. We know that Colorado hates touching poles. Now that he's had a refresher, let's see if the grid did the trick and reminded him of that."

Lani nodded and turned her pony back towards the grid. This time she was ready when he surged forward, half-halting strongly to steady his pace. "Easy, boy," she murmured.

Ms Carmichael was right. Colorado seemed to

remember his training this time. He jumped in neatly over the crossrail and landed at a quiet, steady canter that brought him to just the right spot for the oxer. One more stride, and he rounded nicely over the vertical.

"Whoo-hoo!" Dylan cried as Lani brought Colorado down to a trot. "Way to recover, guys!"

Ms Carmichael laughed. "Good job, Lani."

"Thanks." Lani patted Colorado as they slowed to a walk. She couldn't resist sneaking a defiant glance in Lynsey's direction. "Guess ol' Colorado's a versatile kind of guy after all."

Tessa went next, followed by Jo-Ann. Both Flight and Quest had little trouble with the exercise. Paris Mackenzie took her turn after that. She was riding her own pony, Whisper. The dainty grey mare had turned in one of the best dressage scores in the event, but the pair had been eliminated on cross-country halfway through the course after having too many stops. Now Whisper was dancing and staring at the grid as if she'd never seen a jump before. But Ms Carmichael talked Paris through it, and by the third try they were sweeping through it easily.

Then it was Dylan's turn. Morello pranced into the trot just as vigorously as Colorado had, but Dylan had obviously learned from watching Lani and the others. She took the spirited skewbald in an extra circle before allowing him to approach the trot poles. After that, Morello settled down and jumped through the grid cleanly, with only a tiny buck at the end to show his high spirits.

"Very good," Ms Carmichael said, which made Dylan grin proudly. Lani didn't blame her. Even though Ms Carmichael was Dylan's aunt, she was very careful not to show favouritism. Any compliment she gave to Dylan was definitely earned. "Honey?" the instructor added. "Want to give it a try?"

Honey looked a bit nervous as she and Minnie entered the grid. But she needn't have worried. Nobody ever would have guessed that Minnie had galloped around a cross-country course just a week earlier. She trotted in and cantered out as calmly as ever.

Finally it was Malory's turn. Lani had noticed that Tybalt had seemed especially agitated throughout the class. During the warm-up, he'd spooked several times, and then later had fought against going on the bit at canter, despite Malory's best efforts. But Lani knew Malory could handle him, so she hadn't thought much about it.

Now, though, she realized that the lean bay pony still looked unhappy. He clamped his tail as Malory pushed him into a choppy, high-kneed trot. They barely made it over the poles without tripping, and Tybalt knocked the crossrail with his front hooves, then ran out before the second element.

"Try it again, Malory," Ms Carmichael said calmly. "See if he'll settle over the poles this time."

Malory nodded, then rode Tybalt back around. But he did no better at the poles, and while he made it over the crossrail this time, he skidded to a stop in front of the oxer, bumping into it and sending the front pole crashing down. That made him toss his head and run backwards into the crossrail, knocking that down, too.

"I'm not sure what's wrong with him," Malory said, managing to steer Tybalt out from among the fallen poles. "He really doesn't want to jump."

Ms Carmichael nodded. "Looks like he's having a bad day," she agreed. "Never mind – if we can have bad days once in a while, our horses can, too. It's forgivable."

"Except when it's the day of a show," Lynsey spoke up. She sighed loudly. "I don't understand why nobody but me seems to realize that Tybalt is just too temperamental for the responsibility of being Junior Jumping Team captain."

"Um, Tybalt isn't the captain, remember?" Dylan reminded her. "Malory is." She snorted. "Or were you imagining him giving pep talks to the other ponies in the warm-up ring?"

Lynsey rolled her eyes. "Grow up, Dylan," she said. "Everybody knows what I meant. That pony is a liability, and there's no denying it. He can't handle the pressure."

At that, Lani spoke up hotly in Tybalt's defence, as did Dylan. Tessa and Paris added their own comments, while Honey and Jo-Ann looked anxious and Lynsey just sat there smirking at all of them.

"Enough!" Ms Carmichael spoke up sternly. "Calm down, all of you. You can practise your lateral work for a few minutes while I set up the next exercise."

Lani steered Colorado into line behind Morello, still stewing over Lynsey's comments. How dare she imply that Tybalt couldn't cope with the pressure of the Junior Jumping Team?

Sure, Tyb has his moments, she thought as she put Colorado into shoulder-in. *But when he's on, he's one of the best jumpers in the barn. Still, it's no surprise that Lynsey can't admit that. Any pony that wasn't imported from Europe and doesn't compete on the A circuit might as well be a donkey as far as she's concerned…*

Colorado bulged his outside shoulder, drifting off the rail and going crooked. Lani tuned back in to him, realizing that she'd better pay more attention to her riding.

Soon Ms Carmichael had finished setting up a single crossrail in the centre of the ring. She asked the riders to canter figures of eight over it, aiming for a steady pace and attractive style. Colorado rushed the first few times, but soon he'd settled into a calmer rhythm. At that point, Lani took a moment to glance over at Malory. She winced when she saw that her friend was still struggling with Tybalt. He was setting his jaw every time she tried to get him to soften, and he remained choppy and short-strided at the canter no matter what she did.

Yikes, Lani thought. *She's really having trouble with him today. Come to think of it, she didn't say a word when Lynsey and Dylan were arguing about him…*

She bit her lip as a new thought occurred to her. Lynsey had accused Tybalt of being unable to handle the pressure of heading up the jumping team. But what if it was actually *Malory* who couldn't cope – in particular, with being team captain? After all, she didn't have much competition experience, and she'd always been more concerned about bringing Tybalt along slowly rather than putting everything on the line to win.

What if Ms Carmichael has given Mal more responsibility than she wants?

Chapter Six

"Here we go!" Lani called, scuffing her toe in the dirt of the batting mound and then smacking the baseball into her well-worn leather mitt. "Just keep your eye on the ball…"

She wound up and threw, forgoing her usual tricky slider in favour of a straight, fairly slow underhanded pitch. Sam was squinting at her from the home plate, the bat held up over his shoulder.

"Swing!" Lani yelled as the ball spun towards him. "Now!"

Sam swung, putting his shoulders into it just as she'd spent the last twenty minutes teaching him. The bat connected with the ball with a satisfying crack.

"Way to go!" Lani exclaimed. The ball popped up into the infield between second and third and she loped after it.

Meanwhile Sam raced for first base, clutching the bat in both hands. Lani picked up the ball and turned back just in time to see him make a dramatic slide into the base.

"OK, that was great," she said with a laugh, hurrying towards him. "But you're supposed to drop the bat before you run. Also, you don't have to slide at first. As long as you touch it with your foot, they can't tag you out."

"Oh." Sam grinned and loosened his grip on the bat. Then he stood up and brushed himself off. "Now that you mention it, I guess you did tell me that. Still, I rather like sliding – feels very dramatic!"

Lani laughed. "OK," she said. "Just don't do it while your dad is watching, OK?" She tossed him the ball. "But that was a pretty good hit. Guess your lucky ball really is lucky, huh?"

"Must be." Sam tossed the baseball from one hand to the other. He'd brought it with him to Chestnut Hill that afternoon in anticipation of his first baseball lesson. Despite his father's misgivings, he'd somehow managed to convince his parents to bring him over the Tuesday afternoon after the game. "Want to switch over to yours for a while?"

Lani glanced at the home-team bench where the Chestnut Hill softball teams sat during their games. Her grandfather's ball was sitting on the bench beside the Gatorade bottle and sweater Sam's parents had insisted he bring along.

"Nah, that's OK," she said. "We need a ball that's lucky for *you*, not me."

Sam looked over at the other ball, too. "You never told me how that one became a lucky ball."

"Grandpa caught it during a playoff game at Yankee

Stadium when he was young. He was really into baseball, so that ball was one of his most prized possessions."

"So he realized you were into baseball too and gave it to you?"

"Yeah. Actually, he left it to me when he died. It was written into the will and everything."

She smiled, feeling a pang of nostalgia as she thought back. Her father had been the one who'd taught her the basics of the game and still drilled her on statistics every chance he got, but it was her grandfather who had taken the time to teach her to *love* baseball. She couldn't remember how many times the two of them had sat in the cheap seats at Wrigley Field during the years her family had lived near Chicago, or at the Metrodome in Minneapolis, dissecting whichever game was going on below them.

"Sounds like your granddad was pretty great," Sam said. "You must really miss him."

Lani snapped out of her memories, realizing that he was gazing at her sympathetically. "Of course," she said. "But enough about that. Life is for the living – so let's play ball!"

They kept practising. Sam was a good student and improved quickly, listening to Lani's tips and incorporating them into each new swing. It was another perfect autumn afternoon, crisp and breezy but bright, and Lani was enjoying herself thoroughly – and she was pretty sure that Sam was, too. It was the off-season, so she'd known they would have the softball diamond to themselves. There wasn't even another soul in sight thanks to the place's rather remote location behind the hockey and track fields. It adjoined a grassy lawn that sloped gently down to a deep, rocky stream.

"OK, you're getting better," she said as Sam hit the ball on to the ground near the third-base line. She ran over and scooped up the ball. "Must be the expert coaching you're getting."

"Must be," Sam agreed. "In fact, I'm so good that I'm getting tired of all these wimpy pitches. You were bragging in the car the other day about your super curving fastball or whatever you called it. So let's have a look!"

"Are you sure you know what you're getting yourself into?" Lani warned, pretending to be shocked by the request. "The patented Hernandez slider has been known to make full-grown men cry."

"I'm not afraid." Sam tightened his grip on the bat. "Lay it on me, Hernandez – unless *you're* afraid of my mighty batting power?"

Lani laughed. "OK, here it comes, champ! Prepare to be awed!"

Despite her playful threats, she kept her pitch fairly sedate, putting only a mild curve on the ball as she threw it. Even so, she was surprised when Sam swung and connected solidly with it, sending it flying out over her head.

"Whoa!" she cried. "Check you out!"

She could already see that the ball was going to be a home run. Shading her eyes against the setting sun, she did her best to follow it as it landed in the grassy area past the outfield.

"Oh, man!" she cried, breaking into a run. "Come on – we've got to get it before it rolls into the stream!"

Sam was already sprinting for first base, but he veered off the baseline and fell into step with her as she ran after the ball. "Sorry, didn't mean to hit it that hard," he panted.

"It's not your fault. That was an awesome hit." She glanced at him as they ran. "See, the sports department keeps planning to put up a fence back there to stop the hits that get past the outfielders, but they haven't had the fundraiser yet to raise the money. So for now, they usually just stick a couple of bat girls out there to chase down the balls before they roll down the hill into the water. Practices are another matter, though." She rolled her eyes, thinking back on far too many pairs of wet socks and shoes from the previous spring. "Coach Carter usually makes whoever she's annoyed with that day wade in to fetch them."

By now they'd reached the edge of the outfield. Lani led the way down the hill at a run. But she could already see that they were too late. She groaned as, just a few metres ahead, Sam's lucky ball plopped into the tumbling waters of the stream.

"Drat," she muttered. "Well, guess I'm going to get wet."

She stepped forward, ready to jump into the stream and grab the ball. But Sam stopped her with a hand on the arm.

"Wait," he said. "It's my ball – I'll get it."

Before Lani could say a word, he jumped down the

bank, landing in the water with a splash. "Whoa!" he cried. "The water's cold!" He bent down and fished the ball out from among the rocks. Then he turned and clambered back up the steep bank.

"Hey, thanks." Lani smiled, offering her hand to help pull him back up to higher ground. "You didn't have to do that."

"No worries." Sam straightened up at the top of the bank. He was standing very close. Suddenly he leaned over and kissed Lani on the cheek. "You're quite welcome."

Lani stepped back as quickly, as if he'd slapped her rather than kissed her. Her hand flew to her cheek.

"What was that for?" she blurted out, startled and confused.

Sam shrugged, staring down at the wet ball in his hands. "No big deal," he mumbled. "I just – you know…"

His cheeks had gone pink, standing out in sharp contrast to the rest of his face, which Lani suddenly noticed looked rather pale. She could see that he was shivering, too. The breeze had picked up and the temperature was dropping as the sun sank lower in the sky.

"Um, listen," she said with a flash of concern as she glanced at her watch. They'd been out on the softball field for almost two hours. "Maybe we'd better go in. It's getting late, and I need to get changed for dinner."

"OK."

They headed up the hill and back across the softball

field, pausing just long enough to pick up Lani's lucky ball and Sam's things. He shrugged on his jacket as they headed towards the main part of campus. There was an awkward silence as they walked. Lani wanted to break it – either to try to return to their earlier easy camaraderie, or to demand exactly what he'd been thinking, kissing her like that – but she couldn't seem to find the words either way.

As they rounded the corner of Meyer dorm and came within sight of Adams' front door, Sam finally shot her a glance. "Listen, Lani," he said. "About that – um, what happened by the stream. I didn't mean anything … er, that is, I wish I'd never—"

"There you are!" Honey emerged from the dorm lobby at that moment with Dylan right behind her. "We were just about to send out a search party – oh, Sam!" Her sunny expression suddenly turned anxious. "What happened to you? You're soaked!"

"He wouldn't stop hitting dud balls, so I tossed him in the pool," Lani joked.

But her heart wasn't in it. For one thing, she couldn't help wondering what Sam had been about to say. Was he trying to apologize for kissing her out of the blue?

I hope so, she thought. *I mean, why would he pull something like that, anyway? We were having fun just the way we were. Why mess it up with that sort of thing … at least so soon?*

Besides that, she was feeling guilty for keeping him out so long and bringing him back wet, tired and shivering. Honey and her parents were so protective of him – she should have remembered that and respected it, even if she didn't necessarily agree with it. Then again, as she glanced at his wan face and shivering arms, she wondered if maybe they didn't know better after all…

Meanwhile, Sam was telling the others what had happened. Honey still looked worried, but Dylan grinned.

"Hey, you can tell us the truth, Sam," she said. "You didn't jump into that stream, did you? Lani pushed you because she realized you're a better hitter than she is."

Dylan, Honey and Sam all chuckled. But Lani couldn't help noticing it sounded kind of forced.

"Come along." Honey put a protective arm around her twin's shoulders. "Let's get you inside and into some dry clothes."

A few minutes later, they were all hanging out in Lani and Honey's room. Sam had borrowed some dry socks, shoes, and trousers from the school nurse, and the colour was already returning to his face. He seemed to have forgotten the stream incident already as he and Honey chatted, catching up on home, family, and other matters.

Dylan listened to the twins' conversation with interest, adding a comment or asking a question here and there. But Lani couldn't help feeling a little left out as she watched and listened.

It's amazing how much Honey and Sam look alike now that his hair's growing again and his skin isn't so pale, she thought. *They're pretty much two peas in a pod – you can definitely tell that they're twins. Their smiles are the same, the way their eyebrows arch sometimes when they talk. They even sneeze the same way!*

She almost laughed as both twins let out a sneeze at that exact moment, one after the other.

"*Gesundheit*!" Dylan exclaimed. "Was that one of those weird twin things – you know, Sam sneezes because he was in that cold stream, and then Honey sneezes because she somehow 'felt' his chill?" She waggled her fingers in a spooky way.

"Not exactly." Sam grinned. "More like one of those twin things where we're both allergic to ragweed. Some pollen must've floated by just now."

Lani watched Honey grab a couple of tissues from the box on her bedside table and hand one to her brother.

I wonder what Honey would think if she knew that Sam tried to kiss me, she thought with a touch of unease. *I mean, Honey and I are best friends. But she and Sam are brother and sister. I know she's kidded about it before, but would she mind if we really did end up liking each other?*

She thought about that for a second, forcing herself to consider the questions honestly. She wasn't sure how Honey would react. Then again, that was no surprise. She wasn't even sure how *she* felt about that kiss! She bit back a sigh. Why did things have to get so complicated with her and Sam? Just being friends was so much more straightforward!

It was almost a relief when Mr and Mrs Harper arrived to pick up Sam. They were concerned when they heard that he'd been in the stream, but when Sam insisted he was fine, they dropped the topic.

"We should get on the road," Mr Harper said, checking his watch.

Mrs Harper nodded. "Thanks for looking after Sam this afternoon, Lani."

Sam rolled his eyes. "Mum! You make it sound as if I need a babysitter."

"You do," Honey retorted. "Remember that time a couple of years ago when you decided to cook dinner for the family as a surprise and ended up having to call the fire brigade?"

Sam herded his chuckling parents towards the door. "You heard Dad," he said hastily. "We've got to go. See you later, girls!"

Dylan laughed. "See you!" she called after them. "And don't worry, Sam – we'll be sure to get the rest of that story from Honey as soon as you're gone!"

"Bye," Lani added, though she wasn't sure Sam heard her.

As soon as they were gone, Dylan headed for the door, too. "Save that cooking story for dinner, OK, Hon?" she called over her shoulder. "I just remembered I promised to bring my history notes so Tessa could copy them. The only trouble is, I have no idea where they are!"

"Good luck," Honey said. When the door closed behind Dylan, she glanced at Lani. "Actually, I'm glad we've got a moment alone. I wanted to talk to you about Sam."

"Oh?" For one crazy moment, Lani was convinced

that Honey knew all about the kiss. Maybe she'd seen it in Sam's face; hadn't Dylan just been talking about that weird intuition twins were supposed to have?

Honey took a deep breath. "I know he seems loads better now than he did last year," she said. "But really, he's still quite weak. The doctors say it will take a while for him to be fully back to normal." She gazed at Lani seriously. "Please – just try to remember that, all right? We should all be very careful not to strain him too much."

Lani wasn't sure how to respond. Honey's face and voice were as friendly as always, but there was a hint of warning in her words as well.

What's the big deal? she thought with a flash of impatience. *Sure, he was sick, we all know that. But as he said himself, it's not like he's made of glass!*

Still, the embarrassment was lingering from bringing him back soaking wet from their batting practice, even if it was Sam who had insisted on jumping into that stream. So she forced a smile.

"No problem, Honey," she said, surprised at how normal her voice came out. "I'll be sure to remember."

Chapter Seven

"OK, Colorado," Lani murmured, shortening her reins as she turned the gelding towards the line of jumps in the middle of the outdoor ring. "Let's see if we can get it perfect this time…"

It was Thursday afternoon, and Lani was putting in some extra schooling during the free period before dinner. The first All Schools League show was on Saturday, and she wasn't satisfied with the way Colorado had jumped in class that week. She figured the practice would do them both good, and Ms Carmichael had agreed, allowing her to do some schooling as long as at least one of the stable hands was working nearby in case of trouble.

So after warming up on the flat and over a single crossrail, Lani had set up a gymnastic consisting of trot poles to a crossrail, followed by a vertical, an oxer and another slightly higher vertical. Ms Carmichael had taught them that this sort of grid helped the ponies learn to adjust their jumping form on course, adapting immediately to whatever type of obstacle came up next.

She sent Colorado forward at the trot and circled, making sure he was on the bit and listening before aiming him at the poles. He pricked his ears as they approached the grid, but his trot stayed metronome-steady. He trotted through the poles as lightly as Minnie or Bluegrass, then popped the crossrail easily and landed at a relaxed, steady canter. Lani grinned. This was more like it!

"Steady, boy," she murmured, looking ahead to the first vertical. She didn't want to take back on the reins and risk Colorado getting annoyed and sticking his head in the air. Instead, she merely squeezed them and sat back, and the pony responded, arcing up and over the vertical and landing perfectly on the other side, where he put in another steady but forward canter stride. A slight squeeze with her calves, and he soared over the oxer.

The last element had given them some trouble the first couple of times through the grid. But this time Lani remembered to keep her balance back as they landed from the oxer. And Colorado reacted just right to her aids, maintaining the impulsion he'd had throughout the exercise while also returning to the bouncier, more collected stride he needed to clear the narrow vertical.

"Good boy!" she cried as they landed. "That was awesome!"

As she pulled up, she heard someone let out a cheer. Glancing towards the rail, she was surprised to see Sam watching her.

"Hey!" she greeted him, riding over. "What are you doing here?"

"Mum wanted to drop off some books she's donating to the library," Sam said. "I decided to tag along."

"Oh. Cool." Lani's heart started beating a little faster. She hadn't been able to stop thinking about that weird moment by the stream. And now that he was standing in front of her, it filled her mind so that she could hardly focus on anything else, even Colorado.

Sam took a deep breath. "Um, I can see that you're busy right now." He waved a hand to indicate the pony and the jump grid. "But I don't have much time, and I was really hoping to talk to you about something…"

"No problem." Lani kicked her feet out of the stirrups and vaulted to the ground. "I was just getting ready to call it quits anyway. Ms Carmichael always says it's good to end a schooling session on a positive note, and Colorado jumped perfectly that last time." She gave the pony a pat, then ran up her stirrups and shot a sidelong glance at Sam, feeling a flutter of nerves in the pit of her stomach. "You can come talk to me while I untack if you want."

Sam nodded and followed her towards the barn. He waited until she had Colorado's bridle off, and the cross-ties clipped to his halter. As Colorado was munching a sliced carrot, Sam cleared his throat.

"Erm, I thought we should talk about what happened, you know…"

Suddenly Lani couldn't stand it a moment longer. She wasn't the type of girl to stand around and wait for someone else to lead the discussion. She'd been brooding over the whole situation for two days, swinging back and forth between fretting over that whole weird kiss situation and feeling guilty and annoyed because Honey and her parents seemed to think she was trying to make Sam sick again. It was way too confusing, not to mention distracting. Maybe it was time to put an end to it.

"Wait," she blurted out, turning away from Colorado with only one side of his girth unbuckled. "Before you say anything else, I've been thinking. The baseball stuff was fun and all, but we should probably keep our distance for a while. I mean, you're still getting better, and that should be your focus right now. You don't need me tiring you out and making you sick and stuff, you know?"

Sam bit his lip. "I see," he said. "Look, Lani. Is this about that – um, you know – the, uh, kiss? Because I'm really sorry if I muddled things by doing that." He shrugged. "Really, it was a huge mistake. I have no idea what I was thinking – I *wasn't* thinking, that's all. We're friends – just friends. And that's how it should be."

You don't have to make it sound like kissing me was the worst thing anyone could do, Lani thought, feeling hurt.

She hid her reaction by hurrying around to Colorado's off side and undoing the rest of the girth. Then she took a deep breath and glanced over the pony's back at Sam as she slung the girth over the saddle.

"Deal," she said. "Friends."

"Good." Sam looked relieved. He stepped around Colorado's head, ignoring the pony as he snuffled hopefully at his clothes, clearly hoping for treats. Sam stuck out his hand. "Shake on it?"

Lani awkwardly shook his hand. Still, she was glad to see him smile with such relief. Even if he so obviously regretted that spontaneous kiss, at least he seemed to value their friendship as much as she did.

He's a great guy who's had a really rough year, she told herself. *I need to do everything in my power to be a good friend to him from now on. We have so much fun together that it's easy to forget what he's been through, but I'm definitely going to be more considerate from now on and remember just how sick he was.*

"I'm glad we talked about this," Sam went on. "And I want to thank you, Lani."

Lani swung Colorado's saddle off his back and set it on a stall door. "For what?"

"For never treating me differently even when I was at my sickest." Sam gazed at her. "You always made me feel like I was still a person, not just a sympathy case."

Lani felt uncomfortable as she wondered if he was thinking about his parents and Honey. "Oh, come on," she said. "I'm sure nobody thought of you that way. They were just trying to do the right thing."

"I know. Still, it was kind of a bummer, you know?" he said. "I mean, here I am, suddenly living in an entire new country. But anytime I tried to talk to family or friends back home, all they wanted to talk about was my health! Totally boring." He chuckled sadly. "I suppose my introduction to American life wasn't exactly the best."

Lani hadn't really thought of it that way. How would

it feel if she moved to, say, Australia, and nobody ever wanted to hear about all the interesting new people and places she was seeing?

"Even my own twin wasn't immune," Sam continued, still sounding rather down. "I mean, she tried, I suppose. Mum and Dad, too. But I can't help thinking that a few years from now, all we're all going to remember about this first year is a bunch of hospital rooms and medical tests."

Lani gasped, struck so hard with a great idea that she almost dropped the sponge she'd just picked up. "Wait!" she cried. "We can totally fix that!"

Sam blinked at her. "What do you mean? Are you going to build a time machine or something?"

"Sort of." Lani grinned at the confused look on his face. "No, really. Why don't we make you a memories book? One that shows what a great time you've had getting to know the good ol' US of A. We can take pictures, and include all sorts of other stuff, too, like ticket stubs from that ball game..."

"... and perhaps a description of my first taste of an all-American hot dog," Sam finished, looking excited as he caught on. "Lani, you're brilliant!"

"I know, what can I say?" She waved the sponge around to illustrate her point. "Seriously, though, it'll be great! We can figure out some more fun new stuff for you to do, too. Whatever you want. Then whenever Honey and the rest finally remember that you're a regular person like everyone else, they'll be able to catch up on what they missed while they were busy worrying about you."

Sam grinned. "I love it," he declared. "Let's do it!"

Lani returned the grin. She'd been half joking when she'd blurted out the idea. But his enthusiasm was infectious. Why not do it? She was sure Honey would love it, too. This way, even if she wasn't ready yet to see her twin as well and ready to experience life again, she'd still be able to share in his excitement someday.

She started to sponge away Colorado's saddle marks, her mind already concocting a plan. "OK, first of all we'll have to get a book – like a photo album, or scrapbook-type thing, I guess."

"I'm on it." Sam nodded. "Mum and I are stopping at the mall on our way home today. I'll slip off and find a scrapbook at the card store while she's busy."

"Perfect. So what else have you always wanted to do since you came to this country?" Lani was already looking forward to the new project. Better yet, any lingering awkwardness over that kiss and the rest of it had disappeared as rapidly as the carrots she'd offered to Colorado after removing his bridle. Friends did fun stuff like this together, didn't they? Which meant she and Sam were definitely friends. Nothing else…

Sam began ticking things off on his fingers. "Well, the baseball game's taken care of – I just need to dig the ticket stubs out of my jeans if Mum hasn't washed them already," he said. "I'd also fancy seeing a drive-in movie, trying a funnel cake, staying up all night, seeing a shooting star." He paused and grinned. "Oh, and doing something totally against the rules! Being ill all the time forces you to be good!"

Lani laughed. "Sounds like a plan."

"Oops, I'm supposed to meet Mum back at the car soon." Sam checked his watch. "We can email each other with more ideas. But listen, Lani – let's keep this memories book a secret, all right? Just the two of us."

"Oh. OK," Lani said.

"I mean it. You can't even tell Honey. I want it to be a big, fun surprise when my family finds out, and I don't think they're ready to see it that way yet," Sam warned. "Promise? Swear on your lucky baseball?"

Lani felt a flash of guilt. She already felt as if she were keeping things from Honey since she'd never told her about that kiss. But the way Sam was looking at her, she couldn't argue.

"Promise," she said. "On my lucky baseball."

Chapter Eight

"Rats! I'm all thumbs today." Malory grimaced as her fingers slipped off the tiny buttons of her detachable collar for the third time. The collar fluttered loose and drifted to the floor of the stable bathroom at Alice Allbright's School for Girls, where Malory was preparing for that day's All Schools League show.

Lani picked up the collar. "Here, let me do it." She pushed Malory's hands away, then quickly attached the collar to her shirt. "There you go! You look great."

"Thanks." Malory shot her a smile, but it looked tight and anxious. She wasn't normally the type of person to show a lot of emotion, but she'd been jittery with nerves since Lani had first seen her at breakfast that morning back at Chestnut Hill. Dylan had claimed to be dying of nervousness about the first big show of her eighth-grade career, but Lani had noticed that she'd still wolfed down a whole stack of pancakes and a side of sausage. Malory, on the other hand, had pushed her food around on the plate and left without eating more than a few mouthfuls.

I know Mal's always nervous before a show – that's normal. But she's crazy freaked out today! Lani thought, doing her best to hide how worried she was. The last thing she wanted to do was make her friend even *more* anxious.

Chewing her lower lip, she watched as Malory shrugged on her jacket and hurried over to the mirror to check her reflection. Lani still hadn't shared her concern that Malory might not be ready for the pressure of being team captain – not even with Honey. Then again, that wasn't the only thing she was keeping from Honey these days...

She quickly pushed aside the now-familiar pang of guilt. There was no time for that right now. Malory and Dylan were both on the Junior Jumping Team, and as usual Lani was ready to cheer them on and give them all the help and support they needed.

Just then Honey hurried into the bathroom. "Is Malory dressed?" she asked breathlessly. "Ms Carmichael wants the team members to be out there walking the course in five minutes, and mounted and in the warm-up ring in fifteen."

"I'm almost ready," Malory said, turning around. "I just need to find my show gloves."

"I'm on it." Lani started digging in Malory's holdall, then paused and glanced at Honey. "By the way, where's Dylan? I haven't seen her since we got here."

"Already out there."

Soon Lani was helping Malory walk her course. She watched as her friend worked out the striding between the jumps, figuring out the fastest route. Dylan was a few jumps ahead of them, her brow furrowed with concentration. After a few minutes of following the two of them around, Lani checked her watch.

"Come on, Honey," she said. "Mal can handle the course walk without us breathing down her neck. And I don't even think Dylan has noticed we're here. Why don't we head back to the trailers and start getting Tybalt and Morello ready?"

"All right. See you in a few minutes, Malory," Honey said.

"Uh huh." Malory didn't even look over. She was staring fixedly at a large oxer as she stepped towards it.

Tybalt and Morello were already plaited and saddled and tied to the trailers. As Lani and Honey approached, Morello barely glanced at them. But Tybalt raised his head, straining the lead rope as he stared at them suspiciously.

"Uh oh, Tyb looks kind of tense," Lani commented. "I hope he settles before it's time to go in the ring."

"Malory will know how to calm him down," Honey said. "She always does."

She stepped up into the trailer's small tack compartment and emerged a moment later holding two bridles. Lani hurried forward and grabbed Morello's.

"Is there a brush in there?" she asked Honey. "Or a rag, or maybe an electric carpet cleaner or something? Because it looks like Morello managed to slobber green slime all down his front legs..."

Despite that, both ponies were spotless, shiny and

standing quietly with their bridles on when Dylan and Malory appeared a few minutes later.

"Thanks, guys!" Dylan said, taking her pony's reins from Lani. "It's nice having private grooms." She grimaced. "I just hope you'll be there to brush me off if I have a panic attack and fall off when Morello canters down to that humongous red-and-white triple bar."

"I noticed that one," Honey said with a shudder. "Looks scary!"

Lani glanced over at Malory to check her reaction to the fence. But Malory was busy tightening Tybalt's girth, her face pale and distant. Lani wondered if she'd heard anything the rest of them had just said.

"How's Tyb doing?" she asked her.

"He's a little tense," she said. "But better than he was this morning. I did some T-Touch and other stuff before we loaded them and again after we got here, and I think it helped."

Lani nodded. Malory had learned some special massage techniques and other alternative methods from Amy Fleming, a vet student who had visited Chestnut Hill a couple of times the previous year. It was those techniques combined with Malory's own determination and patience that had helped the highly strung pony settle in and get used to his new job.

"Well, good luck, you two," Lani said. "Anyone need a leg up?"

"Thanks." Dylan quickly checked her girth and then lifted her left leg, waiting for Lani to swing her aboard.

Meanwhile, Honey stepped towards Malory. Before

she could get there, Malory had mounted from the ground. Without another glance at her friends, she rode the sidestepping gelding towards the ring, murmuring soothingly to him.

"Wow," Lani said. "Mal's really lost in her own world right now."

"She'll be OK." Dylan adjusted her gloves as she shot a glance at Malory and Tybalt. "Riding always settles her down."

"True enough," Honey agreed. "Good luck, Dylan!"

"Yeah. Knock 'em dead, Walsh," Lani added. But she couldn't help feeling a little distracted herself as she watched Malory disappear over the rise just ahead.

A few minutes later, she and Honey had found a spot on the rail of the warm-up ring near the rest of the Chestnut Hill students who had come along to watch. Among them was Alyssa Macleod, a seventh-grader from Walker dorm. Alyssa's twin sister, Sienna, was a hotshot A-circuit rider and a member of the Junior Jumping Team at Alice Allbright's.

"Yo, Sienna!" Alyssa called, waving at her sister as she rode by. "Max's boot is twisted. You'd better fix it before you go in."

"Oops, thanks!" Sienna pulled to the centre of the ring and hopped off immediately, bending down to fix her glossy, muscular bay warmblood-cross pony's jumping boot.

"Hey, Alyssa!" Lani protested, only half joking. "No giving tips to the competition!"

"Oops!" Alyssa clapped her hand over her mouth.

As Alyssa's seventh-grade friends threatened to gag her with Vetrap if she didn't stop helping the other teams, Lani returned her attention to the warm-up. Lynsey and Bluegrass looked cool and professional as always as they warmed up with some trot circles and figures of eight. Morello was tossing his head and bucking his way into the canter, but that was normal for him on show days, and Lani knew it wouldn't phase Dylan one bit. The two seventh-graders on the team, Lucy Price and the reserve rider, Joanna Boardman, looked anxious.

"This is soooo stressful!" Lucy wailed as Shamrock tossed her head, almost ripping the reins out of her hands.

Lani glanced at Malory, who was at the rail nearby adjusting her stirrups. But Malory didn't seem to be paying attention.

"It's OK, Luce," Lani called out. "Just picture all the other schools' horses wearing nothing but their underwear."

Lucy looked confused, but Joanna laughed. "Very funny, Lani!" she said. But she was still smiling as she asked her pony to trot.

Seeing that Lucy still seemed freaked out, Lani scooted around the outside of the ring until she was opposite Malory and Tybalt. "Yo, Mal," she said in a low voice. "Meltdown in seventh grade. I think Lucy could use a pep talk from her esteemed team captain."

"Huh?" Malory looked up, then glanced over at Lucy. "Oh. Um, OK." She rode over to the younger girl. "Uh, doing all right so far?"

"Not even a little!" Lucy cried. "Shamrock won't go on the bit, like, *at all*! What's wrong with her?"

"She'll be OK." Malory chewed her lip as the grey mare laid her ears back at Tybalt, making him leap backwards. Malory shortened her reins and nudged him back to Shamrock. "She's just picking up on your nerves. Um, try to use some of those breathing exercises Ms Carmichael taught you. And just be sure to keep her in front of your leg so she can't put her head down."

"That's right," Lani put in. "Kick her butt! You'll be fine."

"OK." Lucy looked slightly calmer. "Thanks, you guys." She rode off around the ring.

Lani opened her mouth to reminisce about how nervous they'd all been as seventh-grade riders the year before. But Malory wasn't even looking at her. The pinched, anxious expression had returned to her face as she leaned down to check her girth one last time. She straightened up and asked Tybalt to walk on.

The dark-bay gelding jumped in the air as if her gentle nudge had been a hard kick, and took off at a rushed, unbalanced trot. Malory eased him back into a steadier trot until he eventually dropped his head. But when she asked for canter, he overreacted again, his hindquarters skittering to one side and almost causing a collision with a rider from Saint Kit's.

Lani winced. "I thought Tyb would be better now that he's back in a familiar setting," she murmured to Honey, who had wandered over to rejoin her. "But he looks just as worked up as he was on cross-country."

"Don't worry," Honey said. "Tybalt is never that comfortable in a crowded warm-up ring, remember? He'll settle once he's out there alone on the course."

"Hope so," Lani said under her breath, though Honey had already turned away to talk to someone on her other side and didn't hear her.

After Bluegrass had walked, trotted, cantered, and popped over a few warm-up fences, Lynsey rode him over to the rail. Bringing him to a halt near the Chestnut Hill contingent, she swung down out of the saddle.

"Hey, Alyssa!" she called. "Come and hold Blue for me. I need to get a drink of water."

Lani rolled her eyes as Alyssa scooted under the fence and hurried over to take Blue's reins. "If that's how Lynsey orders people around when she's *not* team captain, I'd hate to see how she'd be if she *was*," she muttered to Honey.

Just then the PA system crackled to life. Elizabeth Mitchell, Allbright's Director of Riding, began by welcoming everyone to the show. "I'm sure we're all looking forward to another year of good riding, good sportsmanship and good competition," she said. "Without further ado, let's kick off the first All Schools League show of the season. First on course will be rider no. 42, Megan Short of Two Towers Academy, riding American Idol."

Rider no. 42, a nervous-looking girl on a chunky dark-bay Morgan, rode towards the in-gate. "Here goes nothing!" she quipped.

"Good luck," Honey called to her.

"Hey!" Dylan said with mock annoyance. "You're not supposed to be wishing luck on the other teams, remember?"

Honey laughed. "So much for that good sportsmanship Ms Mitchell was just talking about, Dylan," she teased.

Meanwhile, Lani stepped towards Malory. "Ready to rock and roll?" she asked as Tybalt clanked the bit against his teeth and jigged to the side.

"Ready as we'll ever be, I guess." Malory smiled tightly. "You might as well go find a good spot to watch," she added. "I'm just going to walk Tybalt around and keep him loosened up until our turn. We're up second."

"OK. We'll be there to cheer you on. Good luck."

Lani grabbed Honey and the two of them headed over to the main ring, where the Two Towers rider had just knocked down the back rail of the imposing triple bar. "Wow," Honey commented. "The course looks pretty tough."

Just then Lynsey swept past, trailed by Patience. She was just in time to hear Honey's comment.

"It's really not that hard for someone who knows what they're doing," she said with a sniff.

"Right," Patience put in. "At least not for anyone who's ever ridden at the big A shows like Lynsey has."

"Whatever," Lani retorted. "All the A circuit experience in the world doesn't matter if you don't leave the jumps up. Speaking of which, aren't you supposed to be out there warming up your pony, Lynsey?"

Lynsey shrugged. "Blue doesn't need much warm-up. He's a pro." She shot a look at Malory, who had just ridden into sight and was sitting on the still-restless Tybalt near the in-gate. "Too bad we can't say that about *all* the horses on our team."

Before either Lani or Honey could reply, Lynsey continued on her way, pushing past a cluster of Allbright's students.

Lani rolled her eyes. "Gee, with that great sense of team spirit, she wonders why Ms Carmichael wasn't begging to make her team captain," she commented.

"Never mind." Honey nudged her with her shoulder. "Look, Malory's coming in soon."

The Two Towers rider had just cleared the final fence on the course. As she circled to slow down, Malory and Tybalt waited at the gate.

"Here comes Tybalt now," Lynsey commented to Patience. They were standing further along the rail, but Lynsey often spoke at a volume that reflected her belief that everyone in the world wanted to hang on her every word. "Let's just hope those treats help him!"

"Which treats do you mean, Lynsey?" Patience asked, stretching her eyes wide.

"Oh, you know." Lynsey smirked. "The special home-made snacks Malory gave him this morning. The ones in that pink Tupperware container she kept in her jacket pocket."

"Oh, right!" Patience giggled. "*Those* treats."

A couple of the Allbright's girls were looking over at them by now. "What are you talking about?" one of them asked curiously.

"Don't pay any attention to Lynsey," Lani advised,

leaning over the fence to talk to them. "She doesn't know what she's talking about. Mal didn't feed Tyb any home-made snacks this morning – just carrots, like always."

"She's right," Lynsey said quickly. "Don't listen to me. It's nothing. Forget I ever said anything at all."

"Lani!" Honey nudged her again. "Pay attention. Malory's up."

Sure enough, Ms Mitchell had just announced Malory's name and number. As Tybalt pranced into the ring, ears pricked and nostrils flared, Lani could see that the pony was still tense. She also noticed that Malory looked paler and more anxious than ever as she urged him into a trot and began her circle.

Lani crossed her fingers as her friend picked up a canter. But it didn't do much good. It was obvious that Tybalt was already fighting her. He shortened his stride as they approached the first fence, a simple vertical decorated with dried corn sheaves. He tossed his head, trying to escape the bit, and then bolted the last two strides, chipping in and bringing down the top rail. He landed already shaking his head again, though Malory managed to get him over the second fence with no more than a tap from his hind hoof.

"Yikes," Lani murmured. "Come on, Mal…"

She held her breath as Malory somehow heaved Tybalt over the next few fences as well. But when they neared the triple bar, the pony's eyes rolled in alarm. He skittered to one side and then the other, doing his best to run out. Malory managed to keep him from doing that, but she wasn't able to prevent him from slamming on the brakes right at the base, throwing her on to his neck.

A gasp went up from the crowd. Lani exchanged a quick look with Honey, but neither of them said a word.

Malory pushed herself back into the saddle. Her expression was grim, but her hands stayed light and her voice soothing as she steered Tybalt back round in a circle and rode at the fence again. This time Lani could see that she was riding more strongly, urging him on with legs and voice.

"Come on, Tyb, you can do it," Lani whispered.

For a second it looked as if the pony was going to stop again. But then he surged forward and cleared the triple bar by a good six inches. After that, he seemed to settle down and had no more trouble until the last jump, where he brought down the top rail of a tall, airy vertical.

"Malory O'Neil of Chestnut Hill, twelve faults," Ms Mitchell announced as Malory gave Tybalt a pat and rode the steaming pony out of the ring. "Next up, Sienna Macleod of Allbright's on Maximum Velocity..."

Lani let out her breath with a whoosh. "Come on," she told Honey. "Let's go see Mal."

They caught up with Malory just outside the gate. She had already dismounted and was rubbing Tybalt's head. Now that they were out of the ring, he looked tired and perfectly willing to stand there quietly.

"Good job, Malory," Honey said. "We could see that Tybalt was having a bad day, but you handled it."

"Yeah," Lani added. "I bet nobody else could've gotten him over even one of those fences today, let alone the whole course!"

"Hmm." Malory had the tight, closed-in look on her face that meant she didn't want to talk about it. Glancing around, she spotted a Chestnut Hill seventh-grader wandering past. "Hey, Katie, would you mind taking Tybalt back to the trailers for me? Dylan's up soon and I don't want to miss her round."

"Sure, Malory." The younger girl took the pony's reins and led him off in the direction of the trailers.

Lani and Honey exchanged a worried look. That wasn't like Malory. She always liked to take care of Tybalt herself, especially after a tough round. They trailed after her as she made her way back to the viewing area and found a seat.

Sienna and her beautifully trained show pony had little trouble with the course, turning in a fast clear round. As they exited the ring, Dylan rode in on Morello.

Lani cupped her hands around her mouth. "Let's go, Walsh!" she called. "Show us how it's done!"

Dylan glanced over with a grin. She waved at them, then returned her attention to her riding as the starting buzzer sounded. Morello picked up a steady canter right away, pricking his ears with interest at the first fence. He and Dylan proceeded to turn in a careful, stylish clear round.

"Whoo-hoo!" Lani cheered as her friend rode towards the gate. She glanced at Malory, who looked slightly happier.

"That should help the team's score," Malory said. She didn't sound a great deal more cheerful than before.

"Don't worry, Mal," Lani said. "We're doing great so far. I mean, you only had twelve faults – not a huge deal."

Malory shrugged, her expression shutting down again. "I should go and see if Joanna and Lucy are ready to go – it's their first team show, after all, and they're probably nervous." She hurried off before either Lani or Honey could say another word.

Both seventh-graders did look anxious as they rode in for their rounds later that morning. But both also ended up turning in respectable and promising rounds. Joanna, who was riding her own pony, an agreeable chestnut Quarter Pony named Calvin, had one rail down at the triple bar and a stop at a spooky rainbow-coloured vertical. Lucy did even better, bringing down only one rail when Foxy Lady spooked at a bird flying through the ring.

Lynsey and Bluegrass were one of the last pairs to go. Their round was clear and as polished as ever.

By then Lani was sitting in the stands with all three of her best friends. Dylan was still dressed in her show clothes, though she'd removed her helmet and gloves and loosened her collar. She finished chugging a bottle of water as Lynsey rode out of the ring, then leaned over and tossed the empty into a recycling bin nearby.

"OK, Hernandez, you're good at maths," she said, wiping her mouth with the back of her hand. "How'd we do?"

Lani was already running the numbers in her head. She had kept a running tally throughout the show, trying to keep track of each school's number of faults.

"Um, if I'm figuring right, I'm thinking we're ... fifth out of six teams," she said, reluctant to share the not-so-great news. "But it's not because we did badly," she added. "The other teams just did really well. That course looked hard, but some horses seemed to like it."

Dylan sighed, then shrugged. "Oh, well. We've got all year to improve, right?" She forced a smile. "And hey – at least nobody fell off!"

Honey and Lani chuckled, but Malory stood up abruptly. "Come on, Dylan," she said. "We should mount up for the prize-giving."

"We'll come with you." Honey stood too. "Lani and I can touch up the ponies' grooming before you go in."

Lani grinned. "Right. You'll be the best-looking fifth-placers ever!"

Even Malory smiled at that, though it looked kind of strained. "Come on, then," she said. "You two can be the ones to put Tyb's plaits back together if he's managed to rub them out on the side of the trailer."

A little while later, all four of them were heading back towards the ring, Malory and Dylan mounted and Lani and Honey walking beside them. The other team members were behind them on their ponies, along with a handful of their supporters. Lani couldn't help smiling as she listened to the two seventh-grade riders chattering excitedly with their friends about completing their first show. She remembered being in that position herself just a year ago, dancing along beside Dylan and Malory after their first show as members of the Junior Jumping Team...

She snapped out of her nostalgia when she noticed Ms Carmichael striding towards them, flanked by Ms Mitchell and a man she didn't recognize. All three adults looked rather grim.

"Hold up, guys," Ms Carmichael said, putting a hand on Tybalt's bridle. Her voice sounded oddly strained. "Uh, Tybalt needs to come with us. They – they want to do a blood test."

"What?" Lani said, confused.

Malory's face went white. "But Tybalt isn't sick," she said.

"Yeah. What's going on?" Dylan exclaimed. When Lani glanced over, Dylan's brow was knitted with suspicion.

"Please, girls." Ms Carmichael held up a hand. "I'll explain later. Right now, we just need Tybalt."

Malory swung down from the saddle. "Can I come along?" she asked Ms Carmichael. "I – I should be able to keep him calm while they draw the blood."

Ms Carmichael nodded, then glanced at the others. "I'll meet the rest of you back at the trailers in a few minutes."

"But the prize-giving..." Honey began.

"I'm sorry." Ms Mitchell spoke up in her firm, clear voice. "I'm afraid the Chestnut Hill team won't be needed at today's ceremony."

Lani was too stunned to say another word as the

adults turned away, heading towards the Allbright's barn. Malory went with them, leading Tybalt.

When they disappeared around the corner, Lynsey shrugged. "You heard her. We might as well go back to the trailers and get untacked." She turned and marched off with Patience beside her, Bluegrass trailing behind them at the end of his reins.

"I don't get it," Lucy said. "Why don't we get to go to the ceremony? And what did they want with Tybalt?"

Lani shook her head. "I have no idea. I've never heard of anything like this at one of our shows."

"I have. But not at one of *our* shows." Dylan's expression was stormy as she glared in the direction Malory and Tybalt gone. "She said they needed to do a blood test. That can only mean one thing. They think Tybalt was drugged!"

Chapter Nine

"Drugged?" Lani echoed in disbelief. "What are you talking about?"

Dylan shrugged. "It happens on the big circuits," she said, still looking angry. "They test a few horses to keep people on their toes so nobody's tempted to cheat."

"But they've never done random drug tests at our All Schools shows before, have they?" Honey asked, looking perplexed.

"Exactly." Dylan gave a tug on Morello's reins. "Come on, let's go put the ponies away, and then we can figure out what to do."

Lani wasn't sure what Dylan meant by that. But she followed along as the others headed for the trailer, her mind spinning. Could this be the kind of random test Dylan was talking about; some new league rule, perhaps? Or had Tybalt been singled out for some reason? But why would that happen? OK, so he hadn't had the best round in the world, but Lani had seen him behave a whole lot worse!

Just as they had finished untacking the other ponies

and loading them on to the trailer, Malory appeared leading Tybalt.

"Mal!" Lani blurted out, rushing over. Dylan and Honey followed.

"What's happening?" Dylan demanded. "What's this all about?"

"I don't know anything," Malory said, sounding weary. "They took the blood and then shooed me away. It was pretty obvious they didn't want to say much while I was there."

Lani glanced around. Lynsey and Patience and the rest of the eighth-grade cheering section had already wandered off back to the ring, where the Intermediate Jumping Team was currently competing. The Senior team members had just finished tacking up their horses and were on their way to start their warm-up. But Lucy, Joanna and several of their seventh-grade friends were standing around staring at Malory as if she'd just grown a second head, or been caught drowning puppies.

"You heard her," Lani told them briskly. "I'm sure Ms Carmichael will let us know what's going on after the show. You guys go back to the ring and cheer on the other teams, OK? We'll help Mal put Tybalt away."

The younger girls seemed reluctant, but they moved off towards the ring. "Good going, Lani. I thought they'd never leave," Dylan said. "Now come on, let's get Tybalt put away, and then we can talk."

As soon as the bay pony was safely stowed in the trailer with the others, they gathered outside. Malory leaned against the wheel well of the trailer, looking as limp as an overused stable rubber. Dylan paced nearby, her boots kicking up gravel. Honey was standing still, looking back and forth between them.

Lani crossed her arms. "OK, time for a powwow. What's going on?"

Honey cleared her throat. "Do you think there's any chance this could be a new rule for the All Schools League?" she asked. "The drug-testing thing, I mean?"

"I thought of that, too," Dylan said. "It's possible, I suppose. After all, it's not as if Tybalt performed suspiciously well."

As soon as she said it, Lani's heart dropped. Judging by the looks on all three of her friends' faces, she guessed the same thought had occurred to them as had just occurred to her.

"No," she said. "He performed suspiciously *badly*."

Honey bit her lip. "Do you really think that could be it? I mean, he didn't crash through every fence..."

"No." Malory sounded completely miserable. "But he certainly wasn't acting normal, either. Normal for *him*, even."

Dylan frowned. "Oh, come on," she said. "Tyb's always a handful, and it's not like he's never hit a rail before. Why would the officials single him out – especially at the first show of the year, when they haven't seen him for months and months? For all they know he could've been hyper because he hadn't left his home stable all summer, or because it was breezy today, or because he'd had too much sweet feed this week..."

Lani gasped. "Or a horse treat!" she blurted out,

remembering that strange conversation she'd overheard earlier between Lynsey and Patience.

"Huh?" Dylan and Malory said in unison.

Honey's eyes widened. "Oh, you're right, Lani!" she said. "But you don't think Lynsey and Patience would actually slip Tybalt something, would they? That would be too rotten, even for them."

"I know," Lani agreed. "Anyway, we all know he was probably just worked up because of the cross-country thing. No, I doubt anyone slipped him anything. But if Lynsey could make other people *think* someone had..." She rounded on Malory, who looked totally confused. "Do you have a pink Tupperware container with you today?"

Malory blinked in surprise. "Actually, yes," she said. "It has my lunch in it. Peanut butter and jelly sandwiches, if it matters."

"Why are you asking about her sandwich?" Dylan demanded, starting to look annoyed. If there was one thing Dylan hated, it was being out of the loop. "What are you talking about, Lani?"

Lani quickly explained what she and Honey had heard at the ring fence earlier. "I didn't think much about it at the time," she said. "I figured it was just Lynsey and Patience talking to hear themselves talk, you know? It didn't even make sense, saying Malory had brought home-made snacks for Tyb."

"It does now," Dylan said grimly. "They were trying to imply that Mal was acting suspiciously around Tybalt, feeding him something to calm him down or whatever."

"So those Allbright's girls heard her – and decided I'd drugged Tybalt?" Malory gasped. Her face had gone completely white. "They must have complained to Ms Mitchell!"

Honey looked horrified. "I can't believe this."

Dylan clenched her fists. "I can. It's *exactly* like something Lynsey and Patience would do. Lynsey has had it out for Mal ever since Aunt Ali made her captain instead of Her Highness. We can't let them get away with it! Come on, let's go and tell Ali what you guys heard."

Lani nodded, ready to follow her.

But Malory shook her head. "Wait," she said. "What's the point?"

Dylan stared at her in astonishment. "What do you mean? The point is to clear your name! And Tybalt's, too!"

"But they've already taken the blood." Malory shrugged. "They'll find out soon enough that it's negative – that'll convince them much more than we ever could. It's not like we have any proof of anything." She bit her lip and stared down at the tips of her boots. "It's probably better if we just let everything blow over and focus on the next competition."

Lani exchanged a glance with Dylan, who looked as puzzled as she felt. Was Malory serious? If someone had accused Lani of something as dreadful as drugging a horse, she wouldn't be able to rest until she'd proved her innocence any way she could.

But Malory isn't me, she reminded herself. *She's so*

funny about being in the spotlight. Maybe she thinks it would be worse to make a big fuss now rather than just waiting and letting the tests prove she didn't drug Tybalt. Just then a terrible thought crept, unbidden, into her head. *Or maybe she doesn't want to make a fuss because it's true – maybe she* did *drug Tybalt. After all, he certainly has been acting out of character today, and it's not like Mal couldn't figure out how to get into the drug cabinet in Ms Carmichael's office, or maybe even put something together with that herbal stuff she got from Amy Fleming...*

She shook her head, dizzy with shock. How could she even think such a thing about one of her best friends – especially Malory? Malory, who was the least concerned of all of them with winning. Malory, who always put the horse's needs above her own.

But that's just it, the little voice crept into Lani's head again. *Maybe she's having trouble handling the pressure of being team captain and was afraid of bombing out today.*

She sneaked a peek at Malory, who was sitting on the wheel well staring at the ground. It *was* kind of odd that she wasn't reacting more strongly to any of this. Anyone who didn't know Malory better might think she was resigned to being found out.

Just then Malory looked up and met Lani's gaze. The two of them stared at each other for a second. "Do you have something you want to say to me, Lani?" Malory asked. Her voice was quiet, the question clearly intended for Lani alone and not Dylan or Honey, who had stepped away to check on one of the ponies tied to a neighbouring trailer.

Lani gulped. She should have realized that Malory would guess what she was thinking – she'd always had an uncanny way of reading people as well as horses.

"Uh, no," Lani stammered. "That is, I was just – you know—"

Malory stood up. "I thought we were friends," she said quietly. Then she turned and walked away without a backwards glance.

It was a fairly short ride back to Chestnut Hill in the school's minibus, but it seemed to take for ever – especially for Lani. Malory hadn't looked at her since their exchange earlier. She spent the entire bus ride sitting in her seat beside Honey, staring out the window with a grim look on her face.

Oh, man, Lani thought miserably. *I've really done it now. Mal's as sensitive as Tybalt – if she thinks I don't trust her, that's it.*

"You OK?" Dylan glanced over at her. "You're being awfully quiet. For you, I mean."

Lani forced a smile. "Sure. Who can get a word in edgewise with all this racket?" She waved a hand towards the group of ninth- and tenth-graders sitting behind them. The Intermediate Team had won their part of the competition, so the general atmosphere was lively.

Dylan nodded. "Yeah," she agreed. "Anyway, I guess there's not much to say until we figure out how to fix this whole mess." She glanced at Malory, then leaned across the aisle to say something to Honey.

Lani slumped in her seat, glad that Dylan and Honey hadn't noticed the tension between her and Malory yet. *But they will. I have to figure out how to fix this, or Mal might never speak to me again. And I couldn't stand that.*

By the time the minibus came to a stop in the Chestnut Hill stable yard, she still hadn't figured out how to deal with Malory. But she'd realized something else. None of this would have happened if a certain someone hadn't stirred up trouble at the show. Lani looked around at the dispersing crowd pouring out of the minibus just in time to see Lynsey disappearing into the barn with Patience.

"Come on," she said in a low voice, pulling Honey aside as Dylan and Malory hurried off to meet the horse trailer, which had just pulled in behind the bus. "I think it's time to have a chat with the gossip girls of Chestnut Hill."

Honey looked worried. "Are you sure that's a good idea?"

"As a matter of fact, it's the best idea I've had all day. Now come on before Mal sees us and figures out what we're doing."

They tracked down Lynsey and Patience in the barn's main tack room. Patience was lounging on a tack trunk picking at her manicure while Lynsey zipped her bridle into its protective nylon bag, which was colour-coordinated with the rest of her stable equipment.

Lani stopped in the doorway, her hands on her hips. "We want to talk to you," she growled.

Lynsey looked up and blinked. "What is it? We're kind of busy."

"Not too busy to listen to this," Lani snapped. "We know what you did today."

"Wasn't that a movie or something?" Patience smirked at Lynsey.

"Shut up!" Lani was tempted to march over and bang their expensive haircuts together, but she resisted the urge. "You know what I'm talking about. You made those Allbright's girls think Malory doped Tybalt."

Patience rolled her eyes dramatically. "If you ask me, she *should* have doped him," she exclaimed. "He was a basket case! What an embarrassment."

"Totally." Lynsey crossed her arms over her chest and returned Lani's stare with her steely blue-grey eyes. "And I can't help it if a bunch of ditzes from Allbright's misinterpreted a perfectly innocent conversation."

Lani let out a snort. "Perfectly innocent? Yeah, right," she said. "You knew exactly what you were doing. Did you and Patience rehearse your little performance?"

"Chill out, Lani," Patience said. "We were just talking about Malory's stupid pink lunchbox, that's all. There's nothing wrong with that."

Lynsey shot her friend an irritated look. Then she returned her gaze to Lani and Honey and shrugged. "She's right. Those Allbright's girls wouldn't even have remembered that conversation if Tybalt hadn't been such a lunatic today ... and if he wasn't the *team captain's* horse."

"Why, you little—" Lani began hotly.

But Honey yanked her out through the doorway before she could get any further. "Drop it, Lani," she advised, dragging her down the aisle. "Fighting with Lynsey won't achieve anything."

"Are you sure about that?" Lani cracked her knuckles, shooting a look back towards the tack room. "Because I'm pretty sure that pushing her down and rubbing her face in a manure pile would make me feel a *lot* better."

Before Honey could respond, Joanna Boardman came hurrying down the aisle towards them. "Have you seen Lynsey?" she asked breathlessly.

"Many times, unfortunately," Lani grumbled.

Honey gestured towards the tack room. "She's in there. Why? Is Blue OK?"

"Oh, sure." Joanne was already heading past. "Ms Carmichael wants to see the Junior Jumping Team in her office right away."

Lani and Honey exchanged a glance. "Come on," Lani said. "Let's go and see what's happening."

Ms Carmichael's office was located at one end of the U-shaped stable block where some of the privately owned horses were housed. Lani and Honey arrived in time to see Malory and Dylan disappear inside along with the two seventh-grade members. A moment later, Lynsey hurried past without even glancing at them and vanished into the office as well, closing the door behind her.

"What do you think that's all about?" Honey wondered. "They can't have the results of that drug test back already, can they?"

"No way. They only drew the blood, like, an hour ago." Lani kicked at a clod of dirt, feeling nervous and impatient and frustrated all at once. "Guess we'll just have to wait to find out what this is about."

An endless fifteen minutes later, the door opened again and most of the Junior team members poured out, though there was no sign of Malory or Ms Carmichael. Dylan spotted her friends right away and hurried over, looking grim.

"Well?" Lani demanded before Dylan could speak. "What did Ms Carmichael say?"

"We were right," Dylan said bluntly. "They tested Tyb because the steward got an anonymous tip that he might have been doped. So that means we won't get any points from today's show until the results of the blood test come back." She scowled. "Aunt Ali says it's a routine procedure, and we should be glad the All Schools League treats our competitions so seriously."

"Poor Malory! Fancy having to wait all that time to be proven innocent." Honey glanced at the office door, which was shut again. "Where is she, anyway?"

"Aunt Ali kept her behind." Dylan shrugged. "I have no idea what she's saying to her."

Lani followed Honey's gaze to the closed door. She realized how crazy she'd been to let herself think, even for a split second, that Malory might be capable of drugging Tybalt. But that didn't necessarily mean there wasn't something else going on...

She cleared her throat. "Do you guys think that

maybe, you know, Mal might be struggling with the pressure of being team captain?"

The other two whirled around to stare at her. "What are you talking about?" Dylan cried, practically spitting fire. "Mal would *never* drug Tybalt!"

"I know, I know," Lani said hastily, raising her hands. There was no way she was letting them know she'd suspected Malory for one nanosecond. But she couldn't shake the feeling that Malory needed their help in another way. "That's not what I'm saying. We all know Lynsey and Patience were behind this." She hesitated, not quite sure how to say what she wanted to say next. But she couldn't keep it rattling around inside her own head any longer. "But what if Tybalt was so hyper today because ... because Malory was so nervous about all the pressure of being team captain? Or what if she *let* him jump badly because she wanted to be dropped from the team?"

There was a moment of shocked silence. Dylan opened her mouth, but nothing came out. Honey recovered her voice first.

"Do you really think she would do something like that?" she asked softly. "I mean, even if she didn't realize that was what she was doing..."

Dylan tugged at her red hair. "She *did* seem extra nervous this morning, and even this past week or so in class," she said, doubt in her voice. "And of course Lynsey hasn't stopped nagging her about being captain, which Mal must totally hate."

Lani took a deep breath. She realized she'd been

hoping her friends would laugh off her theories, tell her she was crazy. But they weren't doing that.

"So what are we going to do?" she asked.

"What can we do?" Dylan blew out a loud sigh. "Whatever's going on with Mal, she needs our support right now. We'll just have to wait for Tyb's blood tests to come back negative. We can figure out the rest later."

Chapter Ten

"I'm really not in the mood for a movie," Malory said as Dylan and Honey dragged her down the hall between them towards the Junior Common Room. Lani was just behind them, a bowl under one arm and a DVD clutched in the other hand.

"But it's one of your favourites." Honey smiled at her, giving an extra tug as Malory tried to slow down.

Lani caught up to them. "Besides, I've got Dylan's secret stash of popcorn," she said, holding up the bowl.

"Right," Dylan added. "How can you resist?"

Malory sighed. "All right," she said, though Lani couldn't help noticing she seemed to be addressing her response more to Dylan than to her. "Popcorn does sound good, I guess. I'm kind of hungry."

Lani winced. She hoped the others hadn't noticed that Malory still wasn't really talking to her. Then again, it probably wasn't obvious yet because Malory wasn't talking much to anybody. After she'd emerged from Ms Carmichael's office earlier, she hadn't offered to tell her friends what had been said, and none of them – not even Dylan – had asked. Instead, they'd hurried off to the dining hall before they were late for dinner. The others had wolfed down double servings of steak fajitas, ravenous after the long day outdoors. But Malory had only picked at her food.

Dylan hurried forward and pushed through the door. "OK, seventh-grade peons," she announced. "Please vacate the DVD player. It's our turn now."

Lani stepped in behind her and glanced around. A handful of seventh-graders were watching a sitcom rerun on the TV. Several other seventh- and eighth-graders were lounging around on the sofas and overstuffed chairs, including some that had come to spectate at the All Schools show that day. Lynsey and Patience were poring over the latest issue of *Vogue* near the window, but both of them looked up when Dylan and Lani entered. And when Malory came in behind them, the pair exchanged a glance and then raised their magazine in front of their faces.

Lani narrowed her eyes. *Are they muttering about Mal behind there?* she wondered. *Well, let them be immature, then. It's all their fault, anyway.*

The trouble was, they weren't the only ones. Some of the seventh-graders were whispering together, shooting quick glances at Malory before looking away. Even Alexandra Cooper, Malory's roommate, was staring at her with a hint of doubt on her face.

When Lani glanced over, she could tell that Malory had noticed all the attention, too. "This is a bad idea," Malory muttered.

"You're right," Honey said immediately. "Why don't we go hang out in our room instead?"

Lani nodded. "Great idea. Dylan has those new songs on her iPod she's been wanting us all to hear."

"Right," Dylan agreed. "Popcorn goes with music, too."

"No thanks. I'm not really in the mood for company tonight." Not allowing enough time for her friends to respond, Malory spun around and hurried away.

Lani's shoulders slumped. She looked over at Dylan and Honey, who looked equally dejected. Could things possibly get any worse?

"Sorry for the late notice, Lani," Mr Harper apologized as he and Sam climbed out of his car in front of Adams the next day. "If you're too busy for a visit today, we could do this another time."

"No problem, Mr H," Lani assured him. "I didn't have anything interesting to do today anyway." She winked at Sam. "Just my English essay, some French verb lists and a chemistry lab write-up. And none of that even comes close to qualifying as interesting."

"Oh, dear." Mr Harper looked alarmed. "We wouldn't want to interfere with your studies..."

"Chill, Dad," Sam said. "She's kidding. Haven't you figured out by now that Lani isn't serious about anything?"

"You're wrong about that," Lani retorted. "I'm seriously impressed that you just told your dad to 'chill'. We'll have you Americanized in no time!"

Sam laughed. Then he glanced at his father, who was still looking uncertain. "Go on, Dad," he urged. "It's fine."

"Well ... all right." Mr Harper jingled his car keys as he glanced from one of them to the other. "I'll pick you up around five-thirty, Sam."

Lani waved as he got back into the car and drove off. It was Sunday right after lunch. Sam had called her about an hour earlier to suggest getting together that afternoon to work on their project. Lani had been glad of the distraction. Things had been awfully tense around the dorm, and she knew they weren't likely to get better until that blood test came back. Though she felt kind of bad admitting it even to herself, it would be a relief to get out of there and have a little fun for a while. Besides, she'd promised Sam she would help him with his memories book, and she couldn't let her other worries interfere with that.

"So?" she said as soon as Sam's father's car was out of sight. "Did you get it?"

Sam had a backpack slung over one shoulder. He swung it to the ground at his feet, bent over and unzipped it. "Ta-da!" he said, pulling out a large, square photo album.

Lani grabbed it and flipped it open. It had large, smooth, cream-coloured pages interspersed with clear plastic photo pages with lots of pockets. The cover was dark blue, with silver letters spelling out the word *Memories*.

"It's perfect!" she said. "Did your mom ask what you wanted it for?"

118

"Nah, she didn't even see it." Sam shrugged. "She made me haul her shopping bag full of books all over the mall. Nice way to treat a weak and weary cancer survivor, right?" He laughed. "So I told her I wanted to look at the Hallowe'en cards at the stationery store, and after I bought this I just stuck it in the bag with her books and she never even noticed it."

"Very sneaky." Lani grinned, feeling a tiny part of the tension of the past twelve hours melt away in the face of Sam's gleeful expression. "Did you find the baseball ticket stubs?"

"Yeah. I brought them, too. I figured we could put them in there today." He stuck the memories book back in his pack. "So what now?"

They started walking towards the lobby doors. "Well, you didn't give me much notice," Lani pointed out. "But I was thinking about your list. Since neither of us can drive, we can't exactly go to a drive-in movie, even if we could find one." She glanced at him. "I'm pretty sure those went out before I was born."

Sam looked disappointed. "Really?"

"But don't worry, I thought of something even better. We can make our own movie!"

"Huh?"

"I borrowed a digital video camera from the AV department," Lani explained. "We can go out and film ourselves, then edit it in the tech lab. So what's your favourite kind of movie? Action, adventure, sci-fi—"

"Horror!" Sam broke in with a grin. "Especially the

old-fashioned American ones. You know, like *The Blob*, or *The Creature from the Black Lagoon...*"

"Or *The Werewolf That Ate Chestnut Hill?*" Lani put in.

Sam laughed out loud. "Perfect! Let's get going. Lights, camera, action!"

A couple of hours later, Lani's stomach ached from laughing so hard. She and Sam had taken their borrowed camera into the woods behind the horse pastures. There, they had taken turns filming and directing each other, and for a few scenes they'd set up the camera on a tree stump or wall so they could both be in the shot. They'd sketched out a basic plotline on the short walk over from the dorm – boy meets monster, boy chases monster, monster chases back – but the script was mostly ad-libbed and more than a bit silly. They'd even ducked under the pasture fences and included the Chestnut Hill ponies in a few scenes, though the equine extras had seemed much more interested in grazing than in acting. Lani wasn't sure if the movie was going to turn out to be a horror movie or a comedy, but either way she couldn't wait to see the result.

"OK, we're getting some good stuff here. Let's keep going," she said after they'd finished a dramatic kung-fu-style fight scene in a clearing. "Run down this path here to the edge of the woods. I'll stand out there and film you coming towards me. Make sure you look really, really terrified – some screaming would probably help, too."

"Got it." Sam headed back down the winding, shady path while Lani hurried in the other direction. She squinted up to see which direction the sun was shining, then set herself up.

"OK, ready!" she called to Sam. She hit the record button and aimed the camera at the end of the path. "New chase scene, take one. Action!"

Sam let out a bloodcurdling scream from within the woods. There was the sound of racing footsteps, then a moment later he burst out of the trees, wild-eyed and dishevelled.

"Help! Help!" he cried, waving his arms in the air. "It's after me! It's after me!"

"What's going on? Are you guys all right?"

Startled, Lani glanced over her shoulder and saw Chloe Bates and Anita Demarco from Granville hurrying towards them. "Cut," she said, turning off the camera. "It's OK," she called to the two seniors. "We're just goofing around."

"No, we're not," Sam put in. "There's a werewolf in these woods! And it's extra-scary, because it looks just like a regular Chestnut Hill eighth-grader except when the moon is full."

The two older girls exchanged a glance. "O-O-OK," Chloe said. "Lani, you've always had a weird sense of humour. Guess your friends do, too."

"Right," Anita added. "Um, we'll keep a lookout for that werewolf."

They turned and headed back towards the pasture. As soon as their backs were turned, Lani grabbed Sam by the arm and dragged him back down the path. They made it about twenty metres into the woods before they both collapsed in paroxysms of laughter.

"D-did you see their faces when you mentioned the werewolf?" Lani gasped out when she could finally speak again. "For a second, Chloe actually looked nervous!"

"True. But was she scared of the werewolf, or the two crazy people telling her about it?" Sam choked out.

Lani hopped up and offered him a hand. "I guess we'll find out during the next full moon."

Sam waved away her hand and climbed to his feet himself. But Lani couldn't help noticing that he did it slowly. A closer look at his face showed her that he was looking kind of tired.

"What now?" he asked, brushing off his jeans. "Want to try that scene again?"

"I have a better idea." Lani popped the lens cap back on to the camera. "We have a lot of footage already. Let's start editing it."

"That media centre is incredible," Sam said as he and Lani strolled towards Adams dorm an hour and a half later. "I hope they have something like that at Saint Kit's."

Lani shot him a smile. She'd almost forgotten that Sam would be starting at the nearby boys' boarding school after the winter break. It was just one more sign that he really was on the mend.

"I'm sure they do," she said. "That place may look like some big old European fortress, but I hear it's got all the mod cons." She looked at him again. "Isn't that how you guys say it in England? Mod cons? I heard that on BBC America once."

Before Sam could respond, someone called their names. Lani looked up to see Honey and Malory hurrying towards them along the path.

"I had no idea you were coming to Chestnut Hill today, Sam," Honey said, a pleased smile on her heart-shaped face. "Then again, it looks like *I* wasn't the one you were interested in seeing." She turned and winked playfully at Lani.

Lani felt her cheeks go red. She and Sam had been having such a fun time all afternoon; the last thing she wanted was to muddy it up with any kind of romance talk. She knew that Honey loved the idea that she and Sam might like each other as more than friends, at least in theory. But after that awkward kiss, Lani wasn't sure that was ever going to happen. She wasn't even sure she *wanted* it to happen. Somehow, romance seemed much easier when it involved other people!

"I'm glad we ran into you guys," she said quickly, not allowing Honey's comments to go any further. "Want to come along and make funnel cakes?"

"Funnel cakes?" Honey wrinkled her nose. "Are those the fried dough things we saw on TV once?"

"Exactly," Sam said, licking his lips. "Don't they sound great? Lani talked your housemother into showing us how to make them."

Lani nodded. "Where's Dylan? I know she loves that kind of gooey fair food."

"She does," Honey said. "But she's at the language lab. If she doesn't pass that French test next week, Mme Dubois told her she's going to make *all* her teachers speak French to her until she improves."

"Oh, well." Lani shrugged. "More for us, then! Come on – are you guys in?"

"Of course," Honey said. "I suppose I have to try funnel cakes sometime."

"Mal?" Lani glanced uncertainly at Malory.

Malory shrugged. "Thanks, but I don't think so," she said, barely meeting Lani's eye. "I've got a lot to do today."

Honey looked surprised. "Oh, but it will be fun!" she said. "And I can help you with that English paper later if you're worried about it."

"No, it's OK. I want to get it over with." Malory turned and hurried off down the path without another word.

Honey stared after her, still looking surprised. "That's odd," she said. "I'd have thought she'd welcome a distraction right now."

"Come on." Lani felt bad about Malory. But she didn't want to let it ruin things for Sam. "Like I said, that just means more funnel cakes for the rest of us."

As they continued towards Adams, Sam told his sister what he and Lani had been doing that day – without mentioning the memories book, of course. "We edited it in the media lab," he finished. "It was really cool! We could rearrange the scenes we shot and cut back and forth so it looked like Lani was chasing me even when we'd shot us each running separately – stuff like that. Oh, and we added music, too. It turned out fantastic!"

Honey smiled. "Sounds like fun," she said. "But after all that running around, are you sure you're up for more activity? We could always do this funnel cake thing another day. You can take a nap in my room if you like."

Lani felt a momentary flash of irritation. She knew that Honey meant well. After all, she'd nearly lost her twin brother to cancer. Lani couldn't even imagine how it would feel if she were in a similar situation with one of her older sisters – and while she was close to them, especially her sister Marta, she wasn't nearly as close as Sam and Honey. Still, it was hard to watch Sam's family treat him as if he were made of eggshell. Couldn't Honey see that the best thing to help Sam finish his recovery was to let him live his life to the fullest? By trying to hold him back so much, Honey and her parents were still treating him like the sick Sam, the one he was trying so hard to leave behind...

But that's exactly why we're doing this book, Lani reminded herself. While still in the media lab, she and Sam had printed out several stills from their epic horror movie to add to the book. And when they'd found a couple of autumn-coloured leaves that had drifted into Sam's backpack in the woods, Sam had decided to press those and add them, too.

Meanwhile, Sam wasn't annoyed at all by his sister's question – or if he was, he was hiding it pretty well. "I think I can manage to stand around a kitchen and stir things," he joked. "And eating – I'm definitely up for eating."

Honey laughed. "All right, all right."

Soon they were knocking on the door of the private apartment near the main doors, where Adams housemother Mrs Herson lived with her husband and their two young children. Lani looked around with interest as Mrs Herson greeted them and showed them in. She'd never been inside the apartment before. Somehow she'd always envisioned the Herson family as being crowded into the same type of boxy, smallish rooms as the rest of the residents of Adams dorm. But in fact the apartment was quite large, with an open, airy design that made it feel very welcoming. The main living area held lots of comfortable-looking furniture in shades of terracotta, leafy potted plants, and shelves crammed full of books. A colourful Oriental rug covered the wooden floorboards, and a sleek grey cat stared at them from its perch on a sunny windowsill.

"Wow," Lani blurted out. "This looks like a real home!"

"Lani!" Honey said, sounding shocked, as Sam burst out laughing.

Luckily Mrs Herson seemed amused rather than insulted by Lani's comment. "Thanks, Lani. We think so too." She chuckled. "Now come along, the kitchen is at the back. But are you sure you wouldn't rather bake some cookies or a nice pie rather than funnel cakes?" She looked hopeful as she led them past a partition to a sunny kitchen area with a cheerful blue tiled floor and white-painted wooden cabinets.

Lani grinned. Everyone in Adams knew that Mrs Herson was an enthusiastic and talented amateur cook who enjoyed trying new and exotic recipes whenever she had the time. It was no surprise that she wasn't terribly impressed with their choice of cuisine.

"Sorry," she said. "It has to be funnel cakes."

"All right then," the housemother said with good humour. "Good thing my husband, David, took Jack and Molly to their soccer tournament today. Otherwise I'm sure they'd all be here helping you."

They gathered around the butcher-block island in the middle of the kitchen, where the housemother had already set out some mixing bowls and other tools. When Sam pulled a packet of funnel-cake mix out of his backpack, Mrs Herson looked horrified.

"Those mixes are awful!" she said. "Wouldn't you rather make them from scratch? I can look up the recipe in my books." She waved a hand at the shelves built into a cabinet near the refrigerator, which were stuffed with dozens of cookbooks.

"Thanks, but we don't want to bother you," Lani said. "I'm sure the mix will be fine."

The housemother still looked dubious. "All right, if you say so," she said. "I'll be in the other room. Call me when you're ready to turn on the stove."

"Somehow, it's not quite what I was expecting." Sam burped, then wiped his sticky hands on a paper towel.

127

The remains of his half-eaten funnel cake sat in front of him on the counter.

"Well, they're not supposed to be that sticky and...gloopy," Lani admitted.

Mrs Herson shook her head. She was helping them clean up the kitchen. "I told you that you shouldn't use that mix," she said. "Next time I'll show you how to make them from scratch."

She tossed the box from the funnel-cake mix into the trash. When nobody was looking, Lani stepped over and fished it out again. Then she passed it to Sam, who stuck it in his backpack. She figured they could add the front panel of the box to the memories book, along with printouts of the photos Lani had taken of the cooking session with her digital camera.

"Um, next time?" Sam looked dubious. "Well, thanks again for letting us use your kitchen, Mrs Herson. But I'm not sure this was an experience I feel the need to repeat."

Lani poked him in the arm. "You should have waited and tried funnel cakes at a fair next spring like I told you."

Sam laughed. "I couldn't wait that long," he said. "I wanted – er..." His voice trailed off, and he glanced at Honey. "I just wanted to try one right away."

Honey shot him an odd look. Lani gulped. She could tell that Sam still didn't want to let his sister in on the memories book.

"He couldn't wait because, um, I told him he had to try funnel cakes as soon as possible to experience real American life," she said quickly.

"Huh?" Honey blinked at her. "But you just said you suggested he wait to try them."

"Hey!" Sam said abruptly. "Speaking of trying things, did I tell you guys about the new TV show I watched last night?"

Lani was relieved for the change of subject. But as the others chatted about their favourite TV series while they cleaned up the kitchen, she couldn't quite manage to focus on the conversation. She still felt terrible for keeping Honey in the dark about the memories book. But what else could she do? She'd made a promise to Sam, and Lani Hernandez always kept her promises.

Chapter Eleven

"Malory?" Ms Carmichael said, sticking her head out of her office. "Could you come in here for a moment, please?"

Lani exchanged glances with Honey and Dylan as Malory nodded and hurried off. The four of them were on their way to riding class on Monday afternoon. Dylan and Honey had spent most of the walk down from the dorm arguing over the answers to their latest French quiz. But Lani hadn't participated much in the discussion. She was too distracted by Malory, who seemed gloomier than ever that day. The longer things went on that way, the more helpless Lani felt to fix them.

"Do you think the blood tests are back?" Honey asked.

"What else could it be?" Dylan bit her lip and stared at the office door. "I wish I had X-ray vision so we could see what's happening in there."

"It's not X-ray vision you need, it's X-ray hearing," Lani pointed out. "But I know how you feel."

"Should we keep going to the barn?" Honey asked uncertainly.

"Are you kidding?" Dylan rolled her eyes. "I can't do a thing until we find out the test results. If I tried to tack up right now, I'd probably end up putting Morello's bridle on his legs and his brushing boots on his head!"

Luckily they didn't have long to wait. A few minutes later Malory emerged. Lani peered at her, trying to read her expression, but as usual, Malory's face didn't give much away.

"Well?" Dylan demanded. "What did she want?"

"The tests came back," Malory said quietly. "They were negative."

"Whoo-hoo!" Honey cheered, while Dylan gave a loud wolf whistle that made the horses in the closest paddock look up in alarm. Meanwhile, Lani sagged with relief.

I wish I'd never, ever suspected differently, she thought, doing her best to catch Malory's eye. But Malory didn't look at her.

"We knew you were innocent!" Dylan said, flinging her arms around Malory and spinning her around. "Anyone who could think you'd ever drug Tyb would have to be insane."

Lani felt a pang of guilt. Dylan was right. How could she ever have doubted Malory, even for a moment?

Ms Carmichael came out of her office. "What's all the commotion out here?" she asked, though from the smile on her face, Lani guessed she already knew the answer.

"So does this mean we get our points for Saturday's competition?" Dylan checked.

Ms Carmichael nodded. "Of course. There's no reason for the league to withhold them now that it was proven we did nothing wrong."

Lani couldn't help thinking that while the team might have *done* nothing wrong, that didn't mean there *was* nothing wrong. Drugs or not, Malory and Tybalt's performances hadn't been anywhere near their usual standard recently.

Dylan seemed to be having the same thoughts. "I just hope the rumours settle down now," she said. "I mean, we all know how catty *some* people can be."

Lani nodded, knowing that Dylan was thinking about Lynsey and Patience and the rest of their crowd. They loved nothing more than some juicy gossip, and they didn't care whether or not it had any basis in truth.

But Malory just shrugged. "It's no big deal," she said. "I'm used to people thinking the wrong things about me. I've learned that the only way to deal with it is to ignore the gossip and stay true to myself."

Lani winced. Had that comment been directed at her?

"Good for you," Honey told Malory. She checked her watch. "Now come on, we'd better get moving or we'll be late."

They hurried the rest of the way to the main barn, where their ponies were awaiting them in their stalls. Lani greeted Colorado with a carrot and some scratches in his favourite spots, then headed for the tack room to get his saddle and bridle. When she entered, the only people there were Lynsey and Patience. Lynsey was gathering her pony's tack in preparation for the coming lesson, while Patience was putting away the tack from the Basic Riding class she'd just finished.

"Ah, it's my two favourite people," Lani greeted them, the very sight of the pair raising her blood pressure instantly. "I'm sure you'll both be thrilled to hear that Tybalt's test results came back, and they're negative. No big surprise there, since we all know what really happened."

Lynsey slung Blue's bridle over her shoulder and stared coolly at Lani. "Too bad," she said. "At least if he'd been drugged there would be an excuse for his pathetic performance the other day." Lani gritted her teeth, wishing she could stomp right over and throttle her. "You might think you got away with your rotten trick this time," she said, barely containing her temper. "But watch your step from now on. Because I'll be watching you."

"Ooh, we're sooo scared," Patience said, rolling her eyes.

"You should be." Lani glared from her to Lynsey and back again. "Because if we ever prove you did this on purpose, you're toast!" She turned and stomped halfway down the aisle before realizing that she'd totally forgotten to grab Colorado's tack.

Lani had hoped that once the good news about the test results sunk in, Malory would stop giving her the silent

133

treatment. Not only did that not happen, but Malory seemed more withdrawn from everyone, not just Lani. She didn't have much to say in her classes or out of them, and Lani caught her many times with a faraway look in her eyes. She also found her down at the barn a couple of times, stroking Tybalt and talking softly into his ear.

Lani crept away each time without letting her friend know she was there. After all, Malory didn't seem interested in hearing anything she might have to say right now. Worse still, Lani wasn't sure what she *should* say. Sure, she could apologize for her moment of doubt. But she suspected that wouldn't fix things, either. It was all just so weird – what was going on with Tybalt, anyway? Why had he backslid so dramatically at the show?

Could it really be because of Mal's nerves? she wondered on Tuesday night as she lay in bed after lights-out. Visions of snorting, jigging, spooking bay ponies drifted through her head, but unlike sheep, they weren't helping her fall asleep. *I suppose it's possible, but it doesn't make much sense. After all, nothing has fazed Mal like this before. Even these past few days while waiting for those blood test results to come back, she's been pretty calm and self-contained. It just isn't like her to panic and let her emotions take over – especially to the point of affecting her pony. And she's the last person to care what someone like Lynsey thinks of her. So why would being named team captain change all that?*

She yawned, feeling sleep finally creep in at the edges

of her mind. Whatever the answer to the puzzle might be, it would have to wait until tomorrow.

Wednesday dawned hot and humid, letting everyone in that part of Virginia know that Indian summer had arrived in full force. In that afternoon's dressage class, all the ponies – and most of the riders – seemed listless and cranky. Even Paris Mackenzie's pony, Whisper, who was one of the best-trained dressage mounts at Chestnut Hill, was reluctant to put in the effort to interpret any of her rider's aids.

"No, no!" Mr Musgrave exclaimed as the little grey mare missed a halt-to-canter transition for the third time, jogging off at a slow trot instead. "You're not listening to me, Miss Mackenzie. I've explained the aids several times now, and it's plain to see that you're not executing them properly."

Paris let Whisper drift to a halt. "Sorry, Mr Musgrave," she said in a voice that was dangerously close to a whine. "She's just not listening to me! Besides, it's really hard to concentrate when I have a headache from the heat."

Colorado and Morello were standing right next to each other, both geldings standing on a loose rein and seeming half asleep as they waited their turns. Dylan leaned over toward Lani and rolled her eyes. "That's funny," she whispered. "Because all her whining is giving *me* a headache!"

Lani smiled, but she couldn't help a flash of sympathy for Paris. She wasn't the most talented rider in their class, but she took her riding seriously and worked hard at it.

Honey had heard Dylan's comment, too, and seemed to be thinking along the same lines as Lani. "When you're feeling ill, it's difficult to give your all to anything," she said softly.

For some reason, her words made Lani think of Sam. He'd been trying his best to have fun lately, but the lingering effects of his illness kept him from doing it to the fullest. That was why he'd missed that home run ball, and why they'd had to cut their practice short when he went into the stream, and why he'd tired so quickly out in the woods...

"That's it!" she blurted out as an idea struck her like a thunderbolt.

Mr Musgrave looked over at her. "What was that, Miss Hernandez?" he enquired sharply. "Do you have something to share with the class?"

"No, sorry." Lani shot him a sheepish grin. Then she turned to her friends, who were staring at her in surprise. "I'll tell you later," she mouthed at them.

Luckily the lesson was nearly over, since Lani was bursting to share her new thought. As soon as Mr Musgrave dismissed the lesson and strode out of the ring, she hopped down from Colorado's saddle and led him over to her friends, who were also dismounting. They huddled in the middle of the ring while the rest of the class led their ponies out.

"Listen," she said urgently, crossing her fingers and hoping that Malory wouldn't take what she was about to say the wrong way. Then again, what did she have to lose? "I had an idea when Honey said how it sucks trying to do anything when you're not feeling well. It made me wonder – has anyone asked *Tybalt* how he's been feeling lately?" She shrugged, feeling herself go bright red. "We all know he's been off his game. Maybe it's because he's not feeling right."

Malory stared at Lani, her eyes wide in her pale face. Then she turned to look at Tybalt. He was pawing at the ground, sending up puffs of dust. His ears were flat back against his head and he was rolling his eyes at Colorado beside him, even though the dun gelding was half asleep.

"You know, you could be right," she said slowly. "Let's put these guys away and then go find Ms Carmichael."

Lani noticed that Malory still wasn't meeting her eye. But she couldn't help a small flicker of relief. It was a start...

Twenty minutes later they were in the riding director's office explaining their new theory. When they finished, Ms Carmichael looked thoughtful.

"Well, Malory," she said, "do you agree that Tybalt could be ill?"

"What else could it be?" Dylan said impatiently. "I mean, he's definitely been acting weird lately."

"Right," Lani agreed. "He doesn't even seem interested in jumping any more, which is strange because he always seemed to enjoy that more than anything. Plus he just seems more irritable and stuff."

Ms Carmichael held up a hand to shush them. "I want to hear from Malory. She's the one who knows him best."

Malory hesitated. "I – I think there could be something wrong," she admitted. "They're right, Tybalt hasn't felt like himself for the past couple of weeks."

"Why didn't you say anything before now?" Ms Carmichael asked.

Malory looked at the ground, shuffling her feet. "Because I thought it was my fault," she said. "I – I was getting so wound up about being team captain, and I figured that had to be affecting Tyb. I mean, he's so sensitive – I thought he was just picking up on my nerves, especially at the show at Allbright's last weekend."

Lani stared at her in dismay. She'd guessed that Malory had been hiding her true feelings. But it was still shocking to hear her admit it. It made her feel worse than ever for suspecting her of anything underhanded, even for a heartbeat.

Wow, Lani thought. *Mal must've been even more freaked out than I guessed if it made her miss the fact that Tybalt was ill! I just wish she could have let us help her...* She felt her stomach clench with guilt. *Then again, why should she confide in me? I'm the one who thought she was a horse doper. At least that's what* she *thinks*.

Malory's face was red and she was wringing her hands together. But she hadn't finished. "I was sure it was my fault we did so badly, and my fault that Tyb had to get drug tested." She shot the riding director a sidelong look. "I was just waiting for you to change your mind about me being on the team at all, let alone as captain."

"No way!" Dylan exclaimed, grabbing Malory in a hug. "Quit being such a dork. You're totally brilliant, and everybody knows it!"

Ms Carmichael chuckled. "I think what Dylan is trying to say is that you shouldn't second-guess yourself, Malory," she said. "You earned your spot on the team, and you earned the title of captain, too. I think deep down you know that, don't you?"

Malory shrugged. "Maybe," she whispered, the pain in her voice making Lani feel more wretched than ever.

"Well, you need to stop listening to what other people say and listen to that inner voice instead," the riding director went on seriously. "The voice that tells you that you *do* deserve to be captain. *And* the one that says there might be something wrong with your pony!"

"I know. I'm sorry." Malory bit her lip. "I hope I didn't make Tybalt sicker by not speaking up earlier."

"Let's not expect the worst before we've even looked at him." Ms Carmichael turned and headed for the office door. "Come on, let's see if we can figure out what's going on with Tybalt."

Soon Lani was outside the bay gelding's stall along with Dylan and Honey. The three of them watched as Ms Carmichael took Tybalt's temperature and checked the colour of his gums. Malory held his halter, patting and talking soothingly to him.

"Well?" Dylan asked impatiently as the riding director stepped back from the pony.

Ms Carmichael glanced at her. "He does have a slight fever," she reported. "Nothing too serious, but combined with what Malory just told me, I think I'd better have the vet out to check him over in the morning. Congratulations, Lani. I think you might have cracked Tyb's problem."

Chapter Twelve

"I still think you should have let Dylan and me confront Lynsey and Patience in the common room last night," Lani grumbled as the girls hurried to the yard the next afternoon. Their other classes had just ended, and they were eager to get down to the barn to find out what the vet had to say about Tybalt.

Dylan nodded. "We shouldn't let them get away with their rumour-mongering," she said. "If nobody ever calls them on it, why should they stop?"

Malory shook her head, looking pained. "Can we not talk about this right now?" she begged. The vet's four-wheel drive was parked right outside the main barn. "I don't care about those two. All I can think about is Tybalt."

Lani bit back a sigh and exchanged a frustrated glance with Dylan. Both of them had been more than ready to rumble with Lynsey and Patience over everything that had happened as a result of their obnoxious, mean-spirited prank. Lani in particular had been eager to go. Not only would it teach those two a lesson, but it might make her feel a little better about the fact that Malory still wasn't really talking to her.

But Honey and Malory had persuaded them to let it drop. It had been pretty obvious that Malory was still feeling anxious about the whole situation, especially Tybalt's potential diagnosis.

The vet, Dr Tracy Olton, was packing up her bag when the four girls burst into the stable. Ms Carmichael was leading Tybalt back into his stall.

"Well?" Dylan demanded. "What's the diagnosis, Doc?"

Dr Olton looked up and brushed her auburn hair out of her face, looking a bit surprised. "Oh, hello there, girls," she said. "I've just finished examining Tybalt."

"Dr Olton thinks Tybalt may have contracted Lyme disease," Ms Carmichael said.

"That's right," the vet said. "The weather has been perfect for ticks lately, and I've seen quite a few cases in this area. But we're going to start Tybalt on the appropriate antibiotics right away and I expect him to be back to normal in a few weeks."

"Really?" Malory sounded cautious. "So he'll recover fully?"

"I see no reason why he wouldn't." Dr Orton straightened up and hoisted her medical bag. "He's young and otherwise healthy, and we caught it in its early stages. His symptoms are still quite mild, really – you should be proud of yourselves for catching it quickly. His prognosis is excellent."

Lani felt relief flood through her. Tybalt was going to

be OK! And Malory could stop blaming herself for not catching it sooner.

"Awesome." Dylan was grinning. "See, Mal? It wasn't you at all. Once Tyb's back on track, you guys are going to be unbeatable again!"

The vet and Ms Carmichael headed outside, but the girls hung around in the barn watching Tybalt nose at the hay in his stall.

Honey leaned on the edge of his door. "It's weird," she said. "If you didn't know better, you'd never guess he could be sick."

"I know." Malory reached over and rubbed the pony's neck. "But he's so sensitive that I guess even a mild illness can throw him off." She sighed. "I just wish I'd noticed it before the show."

"Don't you dare beat yourself up over this, Mal," Dylan said. "You take awesome care of Tybalt, and everyone knows it."

"She's right." Honey nodded. "And now you know what's wrong, you'll be able to help nurse him back to health in no time."

Malory cracked the first smile Lani had seen from her in days. "Thanks."

But she turned sombre again as soon as she looked back at Tybalt. Lani bit her lip, wishing she could say something that would wipe that anxious look out of Malory's eyes. But she didn't quite dare to speak up and find out that Malory wasn't interested in hearing what she had to say. Instead she just stood there listening to Dylan and Honey comfort Malory, wondering with a pang if things would ever go back to normal between them.

"Go, Mal! Now that's what I call riding!" Dylan called out.

Lani let out a loud sigh of relief, making Colorado raise his head and flick his ears back at her. Ms Carmichael had assigned Malory to ride Skylark in class while Tybalt began his recovery, and after one false start, the two of them had jumped cleanly around the fairly tricky course the riding director had set up for the class. The spirited chestnut had once been a competitive pony jumper on the A circuit, and could sometimes be a real handful. She'd been Lani's mount for her very first riding assessment at Chestnut Hill the previous fall, and Lani still remembered how hard she'd had to work to get her around. But Malory had just made Skylark look easy!

Thank goodness, Lani thought as Malory rode Skylark back towards the others. *For a second there, I thought Mal really had lost her confidence. But I guess she found it again.*

"Great job, Malory!" Honey called out. "You two looked great."

"Geez," Lynsey said. "You'd think she'd just won the Grand Prix or something, not found her way over a few three-foot jumps without knocking them down."

"Sour grapes much, Lynsey?" Dylan beamed at her. "We're just happy that Mal's back on track, that's all. Shouldn't you be happy, too – you know, for the good of the team?"

"Whatever," Lynsey muttered, gathering up Blue's reins and moving him away a few steps.

Lani watched as Malory brought Skylark to a halt and shot Dylan and Honey a smile. But her gaze didn't quite extend to Lani.

That's it, Lani thought, her anxiety and helplessness about the whole situation finally spilling over into determination. *Enough is enough. Mal and I need to talk this out whether she likes it or not. Otherwise I'm going to go crazy!*

After class was over, Lani waited until Honey and Dylan went to put their tack away. Then she hurried over to Skylark's stall.

"Hi," she said to Malory, who had just removed Skylark's saddle. "Need some help? I can take off her boots for you if you want."

Malory shot her a look. For a second she didn't respond. Then she shrugged. "OK, if you want," she said.

Lani almost smiled. That was more than Malory had said directly to her in days! "I'm on it," she said, ducking under the stall guard. She moved down the pony's side, keeping a hand on the mare to let her know where she was. "Here we go, Skylark. Let me just get these things off you..."

When she straightened up, boot in hand, she found Malory staring at her. Malory looked away quickly, but Lani stepped forward.

"Hey," she said. "Listen, Mal. I'm sorry."

"Sorry for what?" Malory's voice was tight, but also held a touch of curiosity.

"For doubting you." Lani took a deep breath. "I admit it. For a second there at the show, I – well, anyway, I was totally wrong. And I'm really, really sorry. Please say you'll forgive me?"

Just behind Lani, Skylark shifted and stepped over to nose at her water bucket. But Lani kept her eyes on Malory's face. There was a long moment of silence.

"You should know better," Malory blurted out at last. "I would never—"

"I know," Lani interrupted. "I have no excuse. I was an idiot. A huge, world-class, horse's butt of an idiot."

She held her breath and waited. She knew that Malory had a tendency to shut down if she felt betrayed or rejected. Would she ever be able to trust Lani again?

Malory's lip twitched, as if she were trying to smile. "That's true," she said. "You have no excuse. But you're not a horse's butt."

"Really?" Lani let out her breath in a whoosh. "Hey, thanks. So does this mean – um, does this mean you forgive me?"

This time both sides of Malory's mouth twitched. "I guess I might as well," she said. "Otherwise you'll just keep after me until I do, right?"

"Right." Lani grinned, relief filling her up and making her feel all floaty, like a balloon being filled with helium. "Thanks! I really am sorry, you know."

"I know." Malory bent down to remove Skylark's other boot. "But I have to admit, you redeemed yourself when you figured out that Tybalt might be sick. How could I stay mad at you after that?"

146

"So – friends again?" Lani asked hopefully.

Malory smiled. "Friends for ever."

"What should we have for studying music tonight?" Honey asked, sitting down at her desk and reaching for her digital radio. It was Tuesday evening, and she and Lani had just returned to their dorm room after dinner. "Top forty again, or do you fancy a bit of hip-hop for a change?"

"It's up to you tonight," Lani replied, doing her best to keep her voice casual. "I've got to hit the library. I just realized I still have three pages to write on that English paper that's due tomorrow. Time for some serious cramming!"

Honey brushed her hair out of her face, looking concerned. "Ms Griffiths said that paper counts for a full twenty per cent of our grade this term!" she said. "All I've got tonight is a few maths problems and some easy French. Why don't you stick around and I'll help you with the paper?"

"Thanks, that's super nice of you to offer." Lani grabbed her backpack and hoisted it over her shoulder, being careful to act as though it were as heavy as it would be if stuffed with books rather than what was really inside. "But I don't want to punish you for my procrastination. Anyway, I'm sure I can get it done – I just need some quiet time to get rolling. Don't wait up!"

She gave Honey one last cheery wave, then bolted for the door to head off any further protest. Out in the hall, she collapsed against the wall for a moment. Lying to Honey made her feel terrible. Was she risking another of her most important friendships by following her instincts? Then again, what choice did she have? She checked her watch and hurried towards the stairs.

A few minutes later she was peering down the deserted country road outside Chestnut Hill's ornate wrought-iron gates. Before long, she spied a set of headlights cutting through the milky dusk. The local bus wheezed to a stop in front of her, letting off just one passenger at the school gates: Sam.

"You made it!" Lani said, raising her voice to be heard over the roar of the departing bus. "Did you have any trouble?"

"Nope." Sam grinned at her. "Like I told you, Mum and Dad are out of town. They think I'm staying at our neighbour's house tonight, and the neighbour thinks Mum and Dad changed their plans and stayed home after all."

He had emailed Lani that morning with this plan. His parents' overnight trip seemed like the perfect opportunity to come over to Chestnut Hill and work on a couple more of the items on his list.

"What better chance will I get to stay up all night?" he said as he and Lani jogged up the long, curving drive, passing a neat line of paddocks on the left in which several horses could be seen as shadowy shapes grazing in the rapidly fading daylight. "Not to mention doing something totally against the rules! That makes two items in one go."

"Three, actually." Lani glanced at him. He looked pale but determined, his eyes bright with mischief. "I checked an astrology website today, and there's a big meteor shower going on this week. Tonight is supposed to be one of the best nights for seeing it. So there are your shooting stars, too."

"Brilliant!" Sam laughed. "See? It was all meant to be. So what's the plan?" A brief expression of concern passed over his face. "Hey, this isn't going to get you expelled from school or anything, is it? Getting into trouble may be on my list, but it's probably not on yours."

"Are you kidding?" Lani said. "I was born to get in trouble. Ask anyone. Now come on – I have everything we need." She patted her backpack. "I brought a picnic blanket and some snacks. Oh, and my camera, of course. We need to record this epic night for your memories book."

"I brought that, too – I figured we could work on some captions or something." Sam hoisted his own backpack. "I also brought some more snacks." He grinned sheepishly. "I wasn't sure what you'd be able to get, and I didn't think staying up all night would be nearly as much fun if we were hungry."

"Cool," Lani said. "I—"

"Hey!" a new voice interrupted. "What are *you* doing out here, Lani? And is that a *boy* with you?"

Lani groaned. "Patience," she said, imbuing the name with all the annoyance she felt. She turned and glared at the girl, who had appeared from behind a line of shrubs. "Just the person I *didn't* want to see."

Patience crossed her arms over her chest and stared at Sam with interest. "Well, no wonder," she said. "You're out way past curfew. I'm sure Mrs Herson would be *very* interested in hearing about that."

Lani was about to panic – Patience certainly wasn't above tattling – when she suddenly realized something. "Hey, wait a minute," she said. "I'm not the only one out past curfew. What are *you* doing lurking around out here, Patience?"

"None of your business," Patience retorted quickly. Then she frowned. "But listen, I was just kidding. I'm not going to tell Herson anything. And you'd better not, either!"

"Well, I don't know." Lani shot a quick glance at Sam, who was keeping quiet. "I mean, sure, if I tattled on you I'd probably get in trouble, too. But after the stunt you helped pull on Mal at the All Schools show, it might just be worth it for me to turn you in even if it means I get busted too." She paused. "Well, *unless*…"

"Unless what?" Patience demanded, sounding a little panicky.

"Unless you lay off Malory, and do your best to get Lynsey to do the same," Lani said. "If you promise that, I just *might* keep this little meeting to myself."

Patience frowned. "Look, this is stupid," she said. "I don't even care about Malory or the stupid jumping team, anyway. It was all Lynsey's idea."

"Good." Lani smiled serenely. "Then it shouldn't be a hard promise for you to make."

Patience hesitated for a moment, clearly struggling

with what to do. Then she shrugged. "Fine, whatever," she snapped. "I'll see what I can do. But only if you swear to stop threatening me and Lynsey. Then maybe I won't tell Mrs Herson I saw you out here."

"Deal." Lani nodded. "So we both agree – this meeting never happened."

Patience scowled, looking as if she wanted to say something else. But then she shrugged again, spun on her heel and hurried off in the direction of Adams dorm.

"Whew! That was close," Lani said when the other girl was out of earshot. "Patience has the biggest mouth on the planet."

Sam grinned. "Masterfully played, Hernandez," he said. "Now come on – we don't want to miss those shooting stars."

Soon they were climbing the hill behind Old House, the majestic white colonial building at the centre of campus. In the distance, lights sparkled from the windows of the cluster of dorms and a few of the classroom buildings at the bottom of the hill, but where they were it was almost fully dark. Lani pulled the blanket out of her pack and helped Sam spread it out on the grass. Then the two of them flopped down, tucked into the snacks they'd both brought, talking and laughing and trying to toss tortilla chips into each other's mouths.

After a while the conversation drifted off and they both leaned back on the blanket, thinking their own thoughts. Lani stared up at the sky, watching for the first signs of the meteor shower and thinking about what they were doing. Patience or no Patience, there was a pretty good chance she was going to get in big trouble for this stunt. Mrs Herson always locked the dorm's doors at ten o'clock, not unlocking them again until six a.m. unless someone needed to go in or out for a specific and approved reason. It definitely wasn't going to be easy to sneak back in without her absence being noticed.

I wish I could have told Honey the truth about what I was doing, she thought, biting her lip. *That way she could have covered for me with Mrs Herson and the others. As it is, if Honey doesn't fall asleep before ten, she'll probably get worried and report me missing in action…*

"Oh!" She interrupted her own train of thought. A brilliant smudge of white light had just streaked across the sky. "Check it out – did you see?"

She turned to see if Sam had spotted the shooting star as well. To her surprise, he wasn't even looking at the sky. He was staring over at her, looking oddly solemn.

"What?" she demanded. Something about his expression made her stomach drop and her mouth go dry with fear. What if his cancer had come back and he hadn't told her?

He reached for her hand. "I was just thinking," he said, his voice sounding a bit husky and shaky. "There's one thing I didn't put down on my list because I was – I was too shy, I suppose."

Lani blinked, not understanding. "Too shy? What do you mean? What is it?"

Even in the darkness, she could see that he was blushing. "Um, it was 'kiss Lani Hernandez'," he admitted.

Lani knew a cue when she heard one. And this was a totally different situation from when they'd been standing soggily by the stream. Without hesitating, she leaned over and kissed him softly on the cheek.

When she pulled away, Sam was smiling. "Hey," he said. "I—"

"Sam? Sam, is that you?" Spinning round, Lani saw Honey hurrying up the hill towards them. "What on earth are you two doing out here?"

Chapter Thirteen

Lani jumped to her feet. "How did you find us?" she blurted out, her face going hot.

Honey stared at her as Sam clambered to his feet as well. "Patience said she saw you two walking up the drive towards Old House," she said. "In case you didn't notice, Lani, the library is that way." She jabbed a finger down the hill.

Lani winced. She couldn't see Honey's expression in the dark, but she could tell by her voice that she was furious.

"Honey, I'm sorry I lied about where I was going tonight," she began. "But I couldn't – I promised… Er, I promised, um…" She let her voice trail off.

"I made her promise not to tell you." Sam spoke up. "So if you're going to be angry with someone, make it me, not her."

"Are you kidding? I'm angry enough for both of you!" Honey's voice was rising in pitch. "Why are you two sneaking around behind my back? Sam, you're my brother! And Lani, I *thought* you were my best friend.

How could you do this to me?" Her voice cracked on the last couple of words. "It's bad enough that Sam was sick for so long and I thought I was going to l-l-lose him. And now – and now this?" With a sob, she turned and raced off down the hill.

Lani was so startled by Honey's uncharacteristic outburst that for a second or two she just stood there frozen. Then she came back to her senses.

"Honey, wait!" she cried, heartbroken. What had they done? She couldn't stand to have another one of her best friends mad at her – not so soon after she and Malory had made up.

"We have to catch her," Sam said. "We need to explain."

He took off after his sister. Lani paused just long enough to stuff the blanket and snacks back in her bag and grab Sam's backpack as well, which he'd left behind.

She caught up with Sam on the path beyond the library. "Which way did she go?" she panted. "Did she head back to the dorm?"

"No. She went that way." Sam pointed to the left.

Lani nodded. "Of course. The stables." She handed Sam his backpack. "Come on, I think I know where we'll find her." There was no way she was letting Honey suffer in silence, the way Malory had done. Lani needed to make Honey understand that she could be trusted, but that she had made a promise to her twin brother that she couldn't break.

Just as she'd expected, they found Honey huddled

in Minnie's stall, her arms around the grey mare's neck. Minnie pricked her ears curiously, munching on a mouthful of hay as Lani and Sam skidded to a stop on the other side of the stall guard.

"Honey, please listen to me," Lani said. "We can explain all this."

"No." Honey's voice was muffled as she buried her face in Minnie's neck. "I don't want to hear it."

Lani bit her lip. This whole time she'd been excusing all the secrets she was keeping, thinking deep down that this wasn't that big a deal. But after Honey's reaction, she suddenly wasn't so sure any more.

I really messed up, she thought, her heart sinking into her sneakers. *Again*.

"Honey." Sam pushed past Lani and ducked under the stall guard. He grabbed his twin's shoulder and pulled her round to face him. "You may not want to listen, but you have to. We weren't trying to sneak around behind your back. We just weren't sure you were ready for what we were doing…" With that, he quickly explained about the memories book.

Lani relaxed with relief. Now Honey would have to understand!

But when Sam was finished, Honey continued to stare at him white-faced. "That makes it even worse!" she blurted out, her voice thick with tears. "Why couldn't you include me in something like that? It's bad enough that I thought you were keeping some secret romance from me. But this – after all we've been through this year, Sam…" She choked back another sob.

"It's too much! I was so scared for you the whole time you were sick, and now that you're better it's like – oh, I don't know." Her blue eyes were brimming over. Minnie turned her nose and nudged at her, and Honey buried her hands in the pony's mane, turning away from Sam and Lani again. "I don't know if I can ever trust either of you again."

"Don't be like that, Honey," Sam said. "Do you think this year hasn't been hard for me, too? And you and Mum and Dad – you've all been great. But now that I'm better… Well, look for yourself." He reached for his backpack, which he'd dropped just outside the stall. Digging out the memories book, he flipped it open. Over his shoulder, Lani could see that he'd been working on it since the last time she'd seen it. It was open to the page about the funnel cakes. He'd pasted the cardboard box front from the mix in the middle and arranged some of Lani's photos around it. There was writing under most of the photos and some at the top, though Lani wasn't close enough to read it.

"Go away," Honey said, staring fixedly at Minnie's neck as Sam stepped towards her again. "You didn't want me to see your precious book before, and I'm not interested now."

"But why can't you understand?" Sam pleaded, shoving the book at her. "I just wasn't sure you were ready for something like this. I thought you needed more time to get over the whole cancer thing. But don't you get it? *I* was ready. I couldn't stand to go on for one more day as if I were still that cancer patient instead of just me again. That's why I wanted to make the book – so I could start living again, doing some of the stuff I used to be afraid I might never get to do."

Honey still didn't look around. Lani could see from her profile that her mouth was set in a grim line.

"Sounds a bit gruesome to me," she said, her voice as cold as Lani had ever heard it. "Like you and Lani are expecting your cancer to return at any moment and so you're tracking all the stuff you want to do before you die."

Sam recoiled as if she'd slapped him. "Fine," he said, for the first time sounding frustrated. "If that's the way you feel…" But Lani ducked under the stall guard herself and grabbed the book out of his hands. She wasn't going to let Honey talk to her twin that way.

"That's the whole problem, Honey," she said bluntly. "For you and your parents, everything always has to connect back to Sam's cancer one way or another. You guys can't stop obsessing over it even now it's over. Why can't you move on? Stop seeing him as a sick person, and just see him as a person again. This person – here!"

She flapped one hand at Minnie, making the well-trained pony take a step back. With her other hand, she shoved the open memories book in front of Honey.

"Quit it, Lani!" Honey cried. "Why can't you ever just stay out of things?"

Lani didn't bother to answer. She could see that Honey was looking at the memories book, really *looking* at it. Hardly seeming to know what she was doing, she took it from Lani's hand. Lani sneaked a peek at Sam. He was standing still as stone, watching his sister.

"You have photos of me in here," Honey murmured, tracing her finger round the edge of one of the photos from the cooking session.

"Of course." Sam's voice sounded pained. "How could I not? You're my twin sister. My – my best friend."

Honey was silent for a moment as she paged through the book. Lani watched her carefully. What was she thinking?

Finally Honey looked up, her eyes moving past Lani to focus on Sam. "Have I really been treating you like a patient instead of my brother?"

Sam shrugged, and the corner of his mouth twitched. "A little bit."

Deciding to give them some space, Lani stepped out of the stall and wandered down the aisle. Colorado was blinking sleepily over his half-door at her, perhaps wondering what she was doing there at that hour and why she hadn't brought him any carrots. She scratched him under the forelock, trying – sort of – not to listen as Honey and Sam talked.

Finally Honey emerged from Minnie's stall with Sam behind her. "If it had to be anyone sneaking around with my brother behind my back..." She shrugged and smiled at Lani. "I suppose I'm glad it was you."

Lani grinned with relief. "Sorry," she said. "Really, I am. You know I'd never do anything to hurt you – well, on purpose, anyway. Knocking over that stack of books on your foot the other day doesn't count."

Honey laughed. "Apology accepted," she said, swiping at her eyes with one hand. "And I'm sorry for flying off the handle just now. It was just so weird, you know? I came so close to, you know, losing him…" She shot a glance at her twin. Then she turned back to Lani and shrugged. "I guess I'm kind of sensitive now if I think someone might be trying to take him away. Even if that's not what they're doing at all."

"I know." Lani smiled at her. "No need to apologize. But totally accepted."

She grabbed Honey and hugged her. Honey hugged her back fiercely.

"Friends again?" she asked.

"Friends for ever," Lani replied, smiling even more broadly as she repeated what Malory had said earlier.

"Good," Sam said. "Now, since Lani's and my big secret plans have been ruined…" He winked at both girls to show he was kidding. "I suppose I'd better catch the next bus home so you two can get back to the dorm before you get in trouble."

Lani glanced at her watch and gulped. "Oops. Too late," she said. "It's twenty after ten."

"Oh, no!" Honey looked horrified. "If we have to knock to get in and explain to Mrs Herson where we've been…"

Sam glanced around the barn. "Well, let's not resort to that just yet," he said. "I might have a brilliant plan…"

"Oh, no!" Honey said immediately. "We're in enough trouble as it is. And we can't risk you getting involved in – oh." She stopped. "Wait. I'm doing it again, aren't I? Being overprotective and all that?"

Sam smiled at her. "Of course," he said. "But don't worry. I don't expect miracles, just so long as you promise to try."

Honey took a deep breath and smiled. "I promise."

"Good." Sam rubbed his hands together. "Now, listen, here's what we can do..."

"Are you sure this is going to work?" Honey whispered, sounding nervous as she tugged at Bella's lead rope to keep the lazy black pony walking up next to her.

"Hey, there are no guarantees in life, right?" Lani glanced over Morello's back at Sam, who was leading a rather lazy thoroughbred gelding named Lucky. All three of them were crossing the broad patch of lawn between the edge of the stable area and the back side of Adams dorm. "But don't worry. If we get caught, I'll take the rap. Nobody will have any trouble believing I tricked you into this, Honey."

Honey didn't look particularly satisfied with that answer. But she just sighed and gave Bella another tug to keep her from lowering her head to the grass.

By now they were almost at the edge of the puddle of light thrown off by the safety lights at the corners of the dorm roof. They all came to a halt; of the three equines, only Morello showed any indication that he wasn't perfectly content to stand there without moving until the end of time.

"Are you sure he'll be all right?" Honey was watching the skewbald pony as he shuffled his feet and then took a step towards the dorm.

"I doubt he'll go far with the other two just standing here." Lani kept her voice low, shooting a glance at the rows of windows facing them. The night was warm, and most of the windows were open. "If he does, he'll only head back to the barn. I told you, we had to use him – everybody knows he's an escape artist. It will be no trouble at all for anyone to believe he staged a breakout." She glanced at Bella and Lucky, who had both lowered their heads to graze, still seeming happy to stand where they were. She stepped over, removed the lead ropes from their halters, and stuffed them into her backpack. "In fact, the only part they might not believe is that these two made it this far along with him!"

Honey chuckled, then looked at her brother. "Are you sure you'll be all right getting home on your own?"

"I'll be fine. The bus is due in fifteen minutes, and I have my cell phone in case of trouble." He winked at her. "But thanks for worrying about me – really. I'll text you when I get home."

"Thanks." Honey hugged him. "See you soon."

"Yeah." Lani shuffled her feet, suddenly feeling awkward as that evening's kiss popped back into her head. Thank goodness Honey hadn't seen *that*. "Uh, bye, Sam. See you – see you sometime."

"Yeah. Bye, Lani." Sam sounded uncertain. He took a half-step forward, but then stopped and lifted one hand in a sort of wave. "See you."

Lani wished she knew what to think about what had happened between them earlier that night. But she would have to figure that out later.

162

She removed Morello's lead rope as well, hoping that he would stay put at least for a few minutes. "You have the carrots, right?" she asked Sam. "And the peppermint? Bella goes crazy as soon as she hears the wrapper crinkle, so that part shouldn't be a problem."

"Don't worry, I'm on top of it." Sam patted his bulging jeans pocket, then made a shooing motion at them. "Go on. And good luck!"

"You too." Lani grabbed Honey's hand. "OK," she said. "One, two, three – go!"

The two of them raced across the light area to one of the clusters of decorative evergreen shrubs that flanked the building's entrance. They ducked between them, pressing up against the dorm's brick wall. The shrubs were tall enough to hide them from anyone who wasn't looking too closely.

Lani held her breath, hoping the plan would work. As soon as they were hidden, Sam was supposed to unwrap that peppermint, which should make Bella whicker loudly with anticipation. Then he would dump the carrots on the ground to distract the other two – particularly Morello – and make them stay put. If all went well, he would just have time to scoot off before someone inside spotted the horses.

"What if the ponies don't finish all the carrots before someone gets there?" Honey whispered anxiously in Lani's ear. "Someone could find them and get suspicious."

"Are you kidding? Those three?" Lani whispered back. "Those carrots will be gone in about two milliseconds."

"All right, what if they finish them too quickly and wander off?"

"We already talked about this," Lani said patiently. She knew it would always be in her friend's nature to worry more than Lani herself did. "In that case we'll just have to reveal ourselves, go after them, and then accept the consequences. It's not worth any risk to the horses. At least Sam will still be able to get away."

Before Honey could respond, the night-time silence was broken by a loud whinny. Lani held her breath again. A few endless seconds passed; just enough time to make her wonder what they would do if this didn't work at all.

Then a voice rang out from one of the upper windows. "Hey, there's loose horses out there!"

Soon the rest of the outside lights came on, and girls came pouring out of the dorm dressed in pyjamas and slippers. Several, led by Dylan and Lynsey, immediately went to catch the ponies and lead them back across the grass towards the yard. But the rest just milled around in front of the building, chattering excitedly. Mrs Herson and the assistant housemother were there, too, urging everyone to go back inside before they woke the whole school.

In all the commotion, it was a piece of cake for Lani and Honey to slip inside and hurry upstairs. Quick as a wink, they changed into their pyjamas and went back down to rejoin the crowd.

"What's going on?" Lani faked a yawn as she walked

up to join her friends Razina and Wei Lin, who were staring across the lawn. Following their gaze, Lani noted with relief that all three of the "escapees" were in hand and following their captors obediently towards the stable area.

"Didn't you hear?" Razina said. "Some horses escaped. Man, Lani, you really do sleep like the dead, don't you?"

She laughed, and a moment later she and Wei Lin drifted off to talk to someone else. Lani grinned, pleased with how perfectly the plan had gone off. Too bad there wouldn't be any photos of this for Sam to put in his book...

"There you are." Malory walked over to her, wrapped in her blue robe. She peered at Lani. "Hey, you don't happen to know anything about how those horses got out, do you?"

"What?" Lani was startled. "Um, what do you mean?"

Malory nodded at Lani's feet. "Well, it's just a little odd that you'd stop to put on socks and trainers before coming outside. And even odder that they're damp and full of straw when they were clean at dinner time."

"Oops." Glancing down at her shoes, Lani realized she'd been in such a hurry to get back outside that she'd pulled her clothes off and her pyjamas on without noticing that she hadn't stopped to change her footwear. "Um, would it help if I told you it was for a good cause?"

Malory laughed. "Don't worry," she said. "Whatever it is, I trust you. You know that."

Lani smiled back at her. "Yeah, I know," she said. "That's what friends are for, right?"